KU-733-222

SW1

ROTHERHAM LIBRARY & INFORMATION SERVICE

R8 6/2/18

WITON
2 7 FEB 2015

KNOWLES
BEEVERS
2 5 MAY 2016

14/5/24
BRI. 11. 5. 24.

HAMER
- 1 MAY 2015

RUSSELL
1 ? JN 2015

EDWARDS
2 1 JUN 2016
Whittington
10/20

Rochester
2 4 JUL 2015

GRE
2/2/23
2 7 MAR 2023
2 1 DEC 2023

1 4 AUG 2015

LOCKER
- 2 OCT 2015

This book must be returned by the date specified at the time of issue as
the DATE DUE FOR RETURN.
The loan may be extended (personally, by post, telephone or online) for
a further period if the book is not required by another reader, by quoting
the above number / author / title.

Enquiries: 01709 336774

www.rotherham.gov.uk/libraries

SPECIAL MESSAGE TO READERS

THE ULVERSCROFT FOUNDATION
(registered UK charity number 264873)
was established in 1972 to provide funds for
research, diagnosis and treatment of eye diseases.
Examples of major projects funded by
the Ulverscroft Foundation are:-

- The Children's Eye Unit at Moorfields Eye Hospital, London
- The Ulverscroft Children's Eye Unit at Great Ormond Street Hospital for Sick Children
- Funding research into eye diseases and treatment at the Department of Ophthalmology, University of Leicester
- The Ulverscroft Vision Research Group, Institute of Child Health
- Twin operating theatres at the Western Ophthalmic Hospital, London
- The Chair of Ophthalmology at the Royal Australian College of Ophthalmologists

You can help further the work of the Foundation
by making a donation or leaving a legacy.
Every contribution is gratefully received. If you
would like to help support the Foundation or
require further information, please contact:

THE ULVERSCROFT FOUNDATION
The Green, Bradgate Road, Anstey
Leicester LE7 7FU, England
Tel: (0116) 236 4325

website: www.foundation.ulverscroft.com

TRAIL TO THE CAZADORES

The five men who set out into the desert, searching for Joe Hennessey's wayward daughter, are bound together by very different motives: from greed for the offered reward to compassion for the young woman. But after an Indian attack results in the loss of his companions — plus his horse and gun — Texas Ranger Duncan is alone. Astray in this vast, hostile terrain, he is wounded and afraid. To top it all, the Indians who took his compatriots may soon return to take his scalp . . .

Books by Mark Bannerman
in the Linford Western Library:

ESCAPE TO PURGATORY
THE EARLY LYNCHING
MAN WITHOUT A YESTERDAY
THE BECKONING NOOSE
GRAND VALLEY FEUD
RENEGADE ROSE
TRAIL TO REDEMPTION
COMANCHERO RENDEZVOUS
THE PINKERTON MAN
RIDE INTO DESTINY
GALVANIZED YANKEE
RAILROADED!
THE FRONTIERSMAN
LUST TO KILL
HOG-TIED HERO
BLIND TRAIL
BENDER'S BOOT
LEGACY OF LEAD
FURY AT TROON'S FERRY
GUNSMOKE AT ADOBE WALLS
THE MAVERICKS
SHADOW OF GUILT
THE HEAD HUNTERS

MARK BANNERMAN

TRAIL TO THE CAZADORES

Complete and Unabridged

LINFORD
Leicester

First published in Great Britain in 2013 by
Robert Hale Limited
London

First Linford Edition
published 2015
by arrangement with
Robert Hale Limited
London

Copyright © 2013 by Anthony Lewing
All rights reserved

A catalogue record for this book is available
from the British Library.

ISBN 978–1–4448–2283–0

ROTHERHAM LIBRARY &
INFORMATION SERVICES

B 5202717 9C

OES463952

Published by
F. A. Thorpe (Publishing)
Anstey, Leicestershire

Set by Words & Graphics Ltd.
Anstey, Leicestershire
Printed and bound in Great Britain by
T. J. International Ltd., Padstow, Cornwall

This book is printed on acid-free paper

*For my good friends
Richard and Evelyn Smith*

1

There were five men who rode into the desert that spring morning of 1873. Five men bound together by unshared motives. The names of the others would be forever branded in Duncan's memory. There was Jason Ironside, undertaker and former hangman; he had now hung up his ropes to concentrate on bounty hunting. He was a big-boned man, well over six feet tall, whose thick-jowled face was the colour of old saddle leather. His eyes had a fierce, brooding look. It was assumed that he would lead the party, though he showed little appetite for the task. There was church minister Enoch Cooper who clutched his Bible as they rode and whose lips seemed constantly moving in silent prayer. He was a tall, thin man with a slight stoop and he wore a long, black frock coat, his habitual garb. Being

1

white-haired, he looked patriarchal and far older than his fifty years. There were the Haycox twins, Dave and Fred, nineteen years old and as alike as peas in a pod, loose-lipped and ready to enjoy the adventure, particularly with the prospect of a reward.

Finally there was Duncan himself, thirty years of age and of Scottish descent. He was a Texas Ranger on assignment to bring an outlaw to justice. There was, behind his grey-steel eyes, a whipcord determination, and a toughness that foretold he would do whatever he set his mind to. The state governor was determined to stamp out crime in the territory and Duncan's mission was to uphold the law.

Mandy had pleaded with him not to go, now that she was his wife and they had baby daughter Lilly. She'd said that his responsibility lay in not risking getting shot each time he left for duty. But he'd promised just one more time, then he'd settle down and turn to farming. The sad thing was, he'd left home in an ill humour.

Duncan and his kid brother Alex had been brought up on army posts. Their mother had died of consumption, and their pa, a colonel, had had immense pride in his sons. But in 1864 their pa had been killed at the Battle of Spotsylvania. In their sadness, the boys had become inseparable. For five years they'd worked as ranch hands on the big JX ranch. Three times, they'd been on cattle drives of 3000 head each, up the Chisholm Trail to the flesh-pots of Abilene, and there they'd 'seen the elephant'. Every experience had been shared and enjoyed to the full.

Then had come the terrible day when Alex was gunned down by bank robbers. He was in the wrong place at the wrong time. Distraught with grief, Duncan had vowed vengeance on the entire outlaw community. To achieve this he'd joined the Texas Rangers and he'd spent his time chasing bandits.

When on furlough, he'd met Mandy, a teacher, and she'd softened the hatred that burned in him. He'd never felt real passion for any woman before, not even for saloon girls who just rolled onto their backs and got it over so quickly. Now everything had changed and he loved Mandy to the depths of his soul.

They were married within a month and baby Lilly had been the fruit of their happiness.

But duty had called. 'Just one more time,' he'd told Mandy, but he carried the memory of her reproachful eyes as he left.

★   ★   ★

Three days before they rode into the desert word had spread that Edward Hennessey, father of the two girls Catherine and Rebecca, was offering $5,000 in reward money for the return of Catherine. She had run off with a wanted outlaw by the name of Joe Vance. Hennessey was infuriated at his daughter's elopement and swore he'd get her home. The fact that assorted lawmen and bounty hunters had been trying to catch Vance for two years didn't deter him. He'd have been after the runaways himself had he not already suffered two heart attacks and the chase might have brought on his demise. Being a retired banker, he was not short of a dollar or two; hence the reward.

Before they set out, they'd assembled on the shaded veranda of the Hennesseys' fine house on the edge of the desert, and sipped the buttermilk Mrs Emily Hennessey and her daughter Rebecca served; that is, all except Ironside, who requested whiskey.

Edward Hennessey was angry, chomping on his cigar. 'I'll bet every damn dollar I've got,' he said, 'that they've high-tailed into the desert.'

'How come you're so certain, Mr Hennessey?' Duncan had asked.

Hennessey glanced at Duncan as if he was witless. 'Because Vance'll never figure there's anybody with enough guts to trail him into that hell on earth.'

Duncan looked at Jason Ironside's big hands and frowned, recalling how he'd sent at least six men swinging into eternity.

Ironside wiped whiskey off his mutton-chop moustache with his thumb. 'I know the desert,' he said. 'I'll find 'em and I'll make doggone sure young Vance is dead meat.' He tapped the butt of his pistol suggestively.

Hennessey removed the cigar from his mouth. 'Kill him if you must,' he said. 'I don't give a cuss. Just bring my daughter back.'

'We must not take life unnecessarily,' the minister Enoch Cooper cut in. 'After I speak to them, Catherine will come home and Joe Vance will repent. It says in the Bible: 'The Kingdom of God is near! Turn away from your sins and believe the good news!''

Ironside wasn't listening. 'I don't need no help,' he said. 'I work best alone.'

'You mean you wanna keep all the reward for yourself.' Dave Haycox

6

opened his big mouth, drawing a menacing glower from Ironside. But Hennessey forestalled any further retort.

'I think it best if you go as a party,' he said. 'Five stand a better chance of tracking them down than one.'

Ironside frowned but offered no further argument, perhaps concluding that he would later dispose of the others when he chose.

So they'd set off, riding into the day's fieriness, and before long their clothing was soaked with sweat. The desert was a land of dry red stone and sand, dotted by clumps of sage, greasewood, bladderweed and spiny cactus, which shimmered in the heat and looked like prancing devils. Two hawks circled in the blue sky. And across everywhere the wind gusted, scorching them. Hennessey had called this place hell on earth and Duncan guessed he was right.

Ironside carried two big canteens of whiskey, which he drank from periodically.

They were all astride grullas, apart from Ironside who rode a big sorrel. Grullas were tough, wiry and sure-footed horses, particularly good in rocky desert.

During the day, Ironside led them to three separate water holes, where they replenished their canteens and refreshed their mounts. It was true: he certainly knew the desert, at least this part of it.

But now that they were hunting Catherine and Vance, it seemed they had little to go on, unless Ironside knew more than the rest of them. He rode at the head of their little cavalcade, setting a pace faster than the others would have chosen. Their quarry had eloped three days ago and by this time their tracks had disappeared.

Fred Haycox drew alongside Duncan and nodded towards Ironside, who was out of earshot. 'He sure looks like he knows where he's goin'.'

'I guess he does,' Duncan said. 'That's if he stays sober. He ain't spoken a word since we started out.'

'How can he be so damn sure where they've gone?'

Duncan shook his head. 'I'll have it out with him at our next stop.' He looked up, noting how the clouds had swept in. The wind was whipping at them, growing stronger by the minute. 'Guess we're in for a storm,' he said.

The minister, Enoch Cooper, had joined them, his face scorched a raspberry red by the sun. Duncan figured he'd never seen him laugh or even smile. 'The Lord will lead the way,' Cooper said, 'just like He led Moses to the promised land.'

Duncan looked at him and asked, 'How come you're on this crazy hunt, Reverend?'

'I was called to save that poor girl from jeopardy,' said Cooper, 'and to redeem Joe Vance's soul.'

'And how about the reward?' Fred Haycox enquired. 'Ain't you in it for the money?'

'Earthly riches don't tempt me,' Cooper responded.

'So you'll turn Hennessey's money down if we bring the girl home?' Haycox persisted.

Cooper looked irritated. 'The church had its roof blown off. I need money for repairs. What will you do with your share, young man?'

'Guess I'll have a right good shindig,' Haycox said. 'Maybe get a frisky little female or two.' He left the reverend shaking his head sadly.

Sand rose about them as they progressed, feeling gritty, like powdered glass between the teeth. Duncan took a swig from his canteen, rinsed his mouth and spat. He pulled his bandanna up over his mouth and nostrils but the grit seemed to come right through it and within a moment things were as bad as ever. Above them, the sky had turned black and the wind had grown so strong it forced the horses to break stride. It whipped off the reverend's hat; it sailed some thirty feet and he was obliged to ride back and retrieve it.

Duncan started to ask himself why

he'd come on this venture, why duty had always had such a strong pull on him. Why did Mandy's reproachful eyes haunt him *so*? And there was little Lilly. He even missed being awakened at night to feed her.

Now, Ironside set a steady course, as if he knew where he was headed, and Duncan guessed the rest of them were glad to tag along, at least for the present.

There were times when they lost sight of each other. The sand swirled about them, causing havoc with the horses, which were nigh played out, and Duncan was mighty relieved when Ironside reined in and allowed the rest to catch up. He muttered something which Duncan couldn't hear because of the wind, but it was obvious he was calling a halt. He led them down into a slight depression, a buffalo wallow, and they all dismounted, letting their mounts turn their rumps to the wind. Duncan took off his bandanna and tied it around his animal's nostrils, hoping it

11

would provide some relief. They all crouched as low as they could, tucking their noses inside their shirts and finding slight shelter behind the horses. Talk was difficult with the elements howling like a thousand banshees above their heads, but there was something Duncan needed to know. He edged over to where Ironside was hunkered, away from the others.

Placing his lips close to Ironside's ear, he shouted, 'How d'you reckon we're gonna track down Vance and the girl?'

For a moment it seemed Ironside wouldn't answer, but eventually he made the effort to speak. 'There's a town, Pinto, southern end of the desert . . . just this side of the Mex border.' He was struggling to make his words heard above the gale's racket. 'I guess that's where he's headed. The girl . . . she would have slowed him down. Maybe we'll catch him before he reaches there . . . maybe not . . . but we've gotta move fast. There's a water hole up ahead . . . maybe five miles. We need to make it by nightfall . . . If only this damned sandstorm would blow itself out.'

Ironside talked confidently, but he seemed to be assuming a lot. They weren't even sure Vance had come into the desert.

Duncan shuffled back to where the others were sheltering and passed on what information he had gleaned. They suffered a miserable two hours before the storm started to subside. As the wind died, Ironside signalled it was time to move out. The horses were in a bad way, panicked by the suffocating sand, but now that the air was breathable again they struggled gamely on. At first the men remained on foot, leading the animals. Presently they were able to take to the saddle. The sky remained overcast, the surroundings cloaked with gloom.

Of them all, it seemed that the twins were suffering the most from the strength-sapping pace that Ironside was once again setting. They tended to drop further and further behind, and several times Duncan rode back and chivvied them into catching up.

The short-lived dusk of the desert was enveloping them as they at last reached the water hole and made a halt.

Even Ironside couldn't see to guide them in darkness and so they made camp. They hobbled their horses, got a small fire going, brewed coffee and fed on the vittles Mrs Hennessey had prepared for them. There was no talk amongst them. They all seemed to have caught Ironside's moroseness. Duncan glanced around at his companions, wondering about their motivations. Ironside: a hard, cruel man lured probably by the prospect of reward money, not only for taking back Catherine, but for killing Vance. The Reverend Enoch Cooper, straining to read his Bible by the flickering light of the fire. He was driven by the desire to prevent bloodshed and maybe earn some money to replace his church's roof. And the Haycox twins. They were unpredictable, but seemed to have started out to gain financial reward and a taste of adventure, although they'd since realized that the mission was more formidable than they'd imagined.

Finally Duncan considered himself. Maybe he'd been crazy to believe he could find Vance and persuade Catherine to return. But now he thanked his lucky stars that Ironside was leading the party. Without him, they'd have stood little chance of success.

That night, as the fire died to embers and the stars were obscured by low cloud, they bedded down wrapped in their ponchos, using their saddles for pillows. Ironside stayed sitting up, sipping whiskey. Duncan was so tired that sleep overtook him almost immediately. He slumbered, completely unaware of the horror that the hours of darkness would bring.

2

It was midnight when Jason Ironside stirred from his bedroll. Cloud obscured the moon and stars, but from the dying embers of the fire he could distinguish the humped forms of his companions. With some annoyance, he noticed that Fred Haycox was missing. Maybe he'd stepped away to relieve himself. Ironside had no wish to encounter him. The reverend was snoring softly and the other two appeared to be sound asleep.

Ironside had decided to strike out on his own. He hated being shackled with company, and the prospect of sharing any reward was abhorrent to him. He gathered up his poncho, hoisted his tack on to his shoulder and crept from the campsite towards where the horses were hobbled. It was here that a shock awaited him.

Firstly, he stumbled over a body and,

stooping down, he grunted with surprise as he recognized Fred Haycox. His head was slanted at a crazy angle; his throat was slit from ear to ear. Then Ironside saw a scurry of movement in the gloom and heard the soft thud of hoofs in the sand. He became aware that his own horse, the big sorrel, now unhobbled, had somebody on its back. Dropping his saddle, he lunged forward in anger, grabbed at the rider's leg, but his hand encountered greased flesh and he lost his grip. He'd seen enough to realize that the intruder was an Indian; he must have killed Fred Haycox, and there was nothing Ironside could do to prevent him from heeling the sorrel into motion and galloping away into the night.

He blasphemed wrathfully. He turned to another horse, slammed his saddle across its back, tightened the girth and fitted the headstall. He then unbuckled its hobbles and swung astride the animal, kicking it hard. He was angered at losing valuable minutes, but had figured he would stand a better chance of catching the thief if he was in the saddle. Soon, however, he found that he had made a bad mistake and his attempts were futile. The darkness was deep, obscuring any sight of his quarry or his tracks. Reining in, Ironside strained his ears to listen, but he could hear nothing apart from the rasping breath of the grulla and the moan of the night wind; these sounds failed to quell his fury. But of one thing he was sure. He would get his horse back come hell or high water.

He didn't wish to return to his former companions and be part of their weeping and wailing when they discovered the murdered twin. He himself didn't grieve for him. The remaining Haycox was loud-mouthed and of little use. The mealy-mouthed sky-pilot should have stayed in his pulpit and never have been allowed to set out on the hunt . . . and as for Duncan, he didn't trust him one iota. He knew their dislike was mutual.

He had no idea which way the Indian had gone. All he could do was sit tight until dawn, when he would seek the familiar tracks of his sorrel.

He waited out the remaining hours of the night impatiently. His whiskey was diminishing rapidly. His fury relented slightly and was replaced by a craving for blood. As the first glimmer of the new day brightened the distant horizon he had enough light to search the ground. It took him an hour to find the hoofprints he sought. He then followed them with infinite care, the trail leading to terrain cloaked thick with saguaro and thickets of prickly-pear cactus. He felt sure the Indian would not have been operating alone and he loosened his Colt in its holster, ready for instant action should he be ambushed. He wondered where the tracks would lead him. He begrudged the time wasted when he should have been finding Joe Vance and the girl, but he assured himself that no man stole a horse from Jason Ironside and lived to tell the tale.

* ★ ★

'Where's Fred!' Dave Haycox was sitting up in his blanket, the empty bedroll of his brother beside him. Dawn was creeping in, but the surrounding terrain was cloaked by mist.

Duncan shook the sleep from his head and looked around. 'And where's Ironside?' he said.

They all were immediately casting aside their blankets and coming to their feet, gazing about. Dave Haycox hurried off, disappearing into the gloom. The reverend headed in another direction. Their voices sounded unworldly in the morning hush as they called for Fred. Duncan went to where the horses were hobbled. He saw that Ironside's big sorrel was gone, but Fred Haycox's mount still remained. He grunted with concern. He struck off through the clinging mist and soon startled a turkey buzzard, which flapped away from him in alarm. Seconds later he discovered what had attracted the bird. Fred

Haycox was sprawled on his back, his head at a grotesque angle. Duncan peered close and groaned.

Duncan hunkered down, an eerie feeling creeping over him. He noted that Fred's blood was still glistening, making a pool in the sand. This could mean one of two things — the fresh bleeding could have been caused by the tearing beak of the buzzard, or it could indicate that the murder had been committed within recent minutes.

He stood up, glanced over his shoulder uneasily, listening for close-in sound, wishing he could see more clearly in the gloom. He could still hear the calling voices of Dave Haycox and the reverend, but now they seemed further away.

He cupped his hands to his mouth and shouted, 'Over here! Over here!'

Within minutes the others had joined him. Dave Haycox cried out in anguish, then fell to his knees beside the body.

Cooper rested his hand on his shoulder and said, 'The Lord gives and the Lord takes away; blessed be the name of the Lord.'

Dave Haycox was weeping now, in long shuddering sobs.

Duncan recalled how he'd felt when his own brother was killed.

Daylight was seeping in, driving off the mist. Duncan paced around, searching for tracks but finding nothing. He returned to where the horses were hobbled. Here, he discovered the hoofprints of Ironside's sorrel, heading southward. They were not fresh. They had been made hours ago. He also realized that one of the grullas had gone.

Presently Duncan returned to where Dave Haycox and the reverend were digging a grave for Fred. He helped them. Dave was still inconsolable. He turned to Duncan and said,

'Ironside did this. I'll get even with him. Somehow I'll get even with him, I swear it!'

Duncan felt equally incensed against Ironside, although why he should have

22

killed Fred Haycox was a mystery. 'Well,' he said, 'we best give chase as soon as possible.'

Even the reverend agreed that this seemed the best course of action. The grave they had dug was not deep but at least it would keep the scavengers away for a while. With gentle hands, they lowered the body into the hole. The reverend dropped to his knees, spoke the words of a prayer:

In the sweat of thy face shalt thou eat bread, till thou return unto the ground; for out of it wast thou taken: for dust thou art, and unto dust shall thou return.

Then the grave was filled in. Dave Haycox marked it with a large stone but it was not possible to inscribe any words. Instead, he swore he would return one day, recover his brother's body and convey it to town for a church burial.

'You must lead us now,' the reverend

said, turning to Duncan.

Duncan nodded but he didn't feel confident. However, the obvious line of action appeared to be to follow the big sorrel's tracks and make Ironside pay for what he had done.

They went to their horses, saddled up and set out into the rising day. The heat rose about them. Dave Haycox was still shedding tears. The reverend followed behind Duncan, relying on his leadership.

⋆　⋆　⋆

Dave Haycox had been riding steeped in the misery of losing his brother. He couldn't believe that he would see him no more. He was paying little attention as they entered an area of thick, high saguaro. Suddenly he heard a wicked hiss like an angry hornet, followed by a yell of pain. Haycox looked ahead, saw how Duncan's horse had panicked and was galloping off. Duncan was clinging on, but there was a tufted arrow sticking in his thigh. Haycox heard the swish of another arrow — and this time it struck the reverend's horse which dropped like a stone, causing its rider to fall beneath it.

Now the air was vibrating with war cries. Haycox's grulla was rearing wildly as more arrows cleaved the air. He snatched his pistol from its holster, but simultaneously he lost his seat in the saddle and was thrown backwards. He hit the ground heavily, aware that his horse had galloped off, complete with his rifle. He had dropped his pistol. Still dazed, he scrambled to retrieve it, then glanced desperately around. The reverend, five yards away, had extracted himself from beneath his horse, his head now buried in his arms as he sheltered behind the prostrate animal. A cluster of arrows was embedded in its hulk. There was no sign of Duncan. His horse must have carried him away from the immediate danger — but he was wounded.

Haycox had no further time for

contemplation. It was a miracle that he had so far not been hit by arrows. The attack was obviously coming from Indians, probably renegade Comanches. Confirming this, he glimpsed movement within the saguaro, a flash of feathers. He blazed off a shot in that direction but his hand was trembling and he doubted that he found his target. The war cries and firing of arrows had ceased, replaced by a threatening silence. Hugging the ground, Haycox edged closer to the reverend, finding a dip in the sand, scooping with his free hand to deepen it. He wished the reverend had a gun; he doubted that prayer would save them in the present circumstances. He wondered how many adversaries there were and if they would surround them. He knew that he and Cooper were pretty well at their mercy, and he had a premonition that his life would shortly end and he would then be with his brother.

Cooper raised his white head. 'Pray, my son, pray!'

They waited, straining their ears for further sound, but they heard nothing. Haycox had been unaware that Comanches had come this far south; however there seemed no other explanation. He wondered what had happened to Duncan. How badly was he crippled by his wound? Had the Indians caught him? He groaned with his conclusions.

'They've gone quiet,' the reverend whispered. 'Maybe they've gone away.'

'I don't think so,' Haycox said. 'I guess they're hatching up something evil.'

Suddenly a crushing weight slammed down on him, driving the breath from his body. He felt the sharpness of a knife against his throat. Cooper had been similarly attacked, losing his Bible. Haycox felt he was being suffocated by the stench of Indian. He tried to twist his gun around, but his attacker grunted and slashed his wrist with the knife, bringing forth blood; the gun slid from his fingers onto the ground. The knife was returned to his throat.

Cooper was struggling, putting up

some sort of fight, but his attacker gradually quelled his efforts. Another Indian stepped in front of Haycox and kicked him in the face with a leathery foot, causing him to slump face down into the sand. He no longer had the will to fight. They'd been completely out-flanked.

Both white men were dragged up and they got their first clear view of their assailants. There were three of them, naked apart from breech-clouts and moccasins; they were copper-skinned, muscular and bandy-legged, their faces daubed with streaks of red paint, their lank, black hair bedecked with feathers. Their speech was unintelligible but their gestures were unmistakable.

Roughly, the hands of the captives were bound behind their backs with thongs of buffalo hide which were drawn painfully tight. Haycox won-dered why they hadn't been slaughtered immediately, then he remembered that Comanches were notorious for tortur-ing those who were unfortunate enough to fall into their hands, tortures like being hung upside down over a fire and roasted alive; or having your belly slit open and your intestines unravelled; or having your eyes plucked out. He couldn't help himself from shaking violently and this brought laughter from the Indians.

He glanced at the reverend, who had his eyes closed, his white hair awry. He appeared completely absorbed in his own reflections, utterly submissive as he was pushed about.

One of the warriors, seemingly the leader, had a rifle and he covered them with this as they were forced to stumble forward. Shortly they paused and the Indians gathered up a few necessities that they had left while undertaking the ambush. Then they pressed forward again.

Haycox had never dreamed that they would encounter hostile Indians when they had ventured into the desert. He guessed the threesome had probably come south from their homelands to rob outlying settlements or ranches.

For twenty minutes they were goaded on, lashed by the quirts the Indians carried. Haycox's throat burned with thirst and, whilst the Indians drank from buffalo horns of water, none was offered to the captives. They wended their way through thick growths of cactus, the shadow of which did little to relieve them from the stifling heat. Once, Haycox tripped. With his hands bound behind his back, he could do nothing to break his fall and he landed heavily, hurting his shoulder. He was shown no mercy but was kicked until, using his knees, he regained his feet. The reverend drew alongside him and murmured, 'Take courage, my son. Trust in the Lord till the last.' And Haycox concluded that for all his apparent passivity, Cooper was a braver person than he.

3

The sun was a brazen orb when they eventually drew to a halt. They had reached a stretch of clearer ground where there was a water hole. The ground around it was green with grass. Here were signs of a rough camp. A further Indian appeared and greeted the others with a wave of his arm. Close by, five horses were hobbled, taking full advantage of the grass, and Haycox grunted with surprise when he saw Jason Ironside's big sorrel amongst them. He was given no chance to ponder on its presence. He hoped that the former hangman had fallen victim to the Indians and been subjected to most gruesome torture. He still blamed him for his brother's death, believing that the worst fate would never bring atonement for his terrible crime.

As Haycox and Cooper waited for

whatever evil punishment lay in store for them, a warrior approached one of the horses and unceremoniously slashed its jugular with his knife. The beast snorted with agony, sunk to its knees and then rolled over, its blood gushing out. It was scarcely dead before the Indian was slicing flesh from it.

The remaining three warriors set upon the captives, cutting the hide binding their wrists and pulling off their clothes and boots, rendering them entirely naked. They were thrown onto their backs with arms and legs extended. Six pegs were then driven firmly into the ground. Their hands and feet were fastened to these so that they were stretched spread-eagled. Further pegs were driven close on either side of their necks, and strong strips of buffalo hide tied from one to the other, so that it passed beneath their chins, tight across the throat. They were thus forced to lie on their backs, unable to move heads or limbs.

Their distress was finally assured as

the Indian who had killed the horse, and was still glistening with blood, came up with two large rocks which were forced beneath them, preventing them from resting down.

They were staked out, bared beneath the scorching sun. The Indians amused themselves, tugging at the reverend's beard, rocking with glee. Presently they became bored and retired to a more shaded spot, lit a fire and proceeded to roast the horseflesh on sticks. It was at this time that both Haycox and Cooper prayed for a quick death.

★   ★   ★

When Duncan felt the agonizing impact of the arrow thud into his thigh, he struggled to remain in the saddle of his panicking grulla, aware that more arrows were passing perilously close to him. Hunching himself low, he allowed his mount to have its head, carrying him clear. He knew his leg was bleeding and the pain throbbed upwards from the wound, creating dizziness in his head. The ambush had taken them completely by surprise. Now he wondered what fate had befallen Haycox and the reverend. The thought that they must have been killed deepened his misery. He glanced over his shoulder, wondering if any of the attackers was pursuing him. He was fearful of toppling from the saddle. Should he fall, he would be easy prey. He devoted all his diminishing strength to clinging on, helpless to restrain his racing animal. He lost track of how far they travelled. Eventually they drew up, the grulla blown. Duncan could no longer stave off his encroaching weakness. His vision began to swim. He slipped from his saddle, hitting the ground with such impact that the shaft of the jutting arrow was snapped, causing him agony. He lapsed into unconsciousness.

The horse briefly stood over him, even nuzzled him in curiosity but then, as it recovered from its exertions, its head jerked up, it emitted a snort and it trotted off.

*   *   *

Duncan opened his eyes, then closed them quickly, blinded by bright sunlight. Pain emanating from his thigh hit him. Recollection of events flooded back to him; he groaned with anguish. He opened his eyes again, looked up. The molten sky was empty, a vast vacuum from which even the hawks had fled. Gritting his teeth, he forced himself into a sitting position. His gaze focused on the arrow stub protruding from his thigh. He touched it with his fingers, worked it back and forth, sucking in his breath at the hurt. He gave up, unable to bear it. After a moment, his hand returned to the stub. There was looseness to it; again he worked it back and forth. He attempted to pull it out. All he succeeded in doing was to bring a flood of blood onto his fingers. He felt sick. He tried once more: this time his fingernails dug into the stub and suddenly he pulled it free, bringing a further gush of blood. It was tipped with stone. He fell back and fainted.

★ ★ ★

For some strange reason Duncan had been back at home on the day Maddy gave birth. She had gone into labour sooner than expected, long before the midwife came. Duncan had died a small death as he heard Mandy's screams, but that hadn't stopped him from helping her, imploring her to push down. She was panting, the sweat shining on her forehead. Suddenly the rasp of her breathing stopped. She unleashed a long howl and he saw the baby's head emerging, then a shoulder, and together they made a supreme effort, Mandy pushing down while he drew the tiny, blood-glistening body out. His hands seemed so clumsy.

The midwife arrived just as he was

cutting the cord. Soon she had the baby wrapped in a blanket. She handed him the feather-light bundle. Duncan opened the blanket and checked to make sure his daughter had the full quota of fingers and toes. Then, satisfied, he held her close, feeling he had never worked so hard in his life and knowing that this was his happiest day ever.

★   ★   ★

When his senses again returned, he sat up. He felt intensely alone, more so than he had done since he lost his brother. His companions were gone, so was his horse, taking with it his water canteen, saddle and rifle. Even the Indians, it seemed, had deserted him. He was lost in the vastness of unfamiliar, hostile terrain. And to top it all, he had been hurt. He cursed aloud.

He had to survive, if only for the sakes of his beloved Mandy and Lilly. He knew he would gain nothing by remaining where he was. Pressing down with his hands, he pushed himself up, taking his weight on his sound left leg. He put his injured limb to the ground, wincing as shafts of pain shot through him, but he stayed upright, ignoring the discomfort, and after a moment he paced forward. He consoled himself with a piece of good fortune. He still had the Colt holstered at his hip and a knife sheathed on his belt.

★   ★   ★

Jason Ironside was excited. The tracks of the big sorrel showed clearly on the ground, and now instinct told him that he was closing on his quarry. He uncorked his last canteen and cursed as he found it empty. He dismounted, ground-tethered the grulla with a lump of rock, and crept forward through the high screen of saguaro. The scent of roasting meat wafted to his nostrils, activating his taste buds, and shortly he heard the guttural murmur of Indian voices. He drew his pistol, checked that it was fully loaded. He had to make every shot count.

Placing his feet with infinite care, he advanced until the cactus thinned before him and he saw four Indians seated around a fire, eating meat. They were blissfully unaware of his presence.

He opened up with a rapid fusillade of lead, thumbing back the hammer, the gun booming like a cannon. He snarled with delight as his heavy-calibre bullets found their mark. The Indians had twisted around, horror stamped across their dusky faces as they were gunned down. Excitement pulsed through Ironside's veins hotter than liquor. He paused, his breath coming in gasps, then he carefully reloaded his Colt. Six shots, he thought, and four men killed . . . or were they? He stepped forward, examining the bodies. Two were still alive. He pressed his gun to their heads and blew their brains out. He stood for a moment, allowing the singing of the detonations to subside in his ears; then he gathered up the chunks of horsemeat that had been discarded by the Indians, dusted them off and wolfed them down.

He saw where the horses were hobbled, his big sorrel included. He also saw the carcass of the horse that had been slaughtered and decided he would slice off a supply of meat before he travelled on. He was about to undertake that task when he heard a low, groaning sound. He turned and with astonishment saw the two figures pegged out on the open ground, their skin blotched red by the sun. Haycox and the reverend, naked as plucked chickens! It was Haycox who had emitted the low cry.

Ironside stepped across, stood looking down at them. Both had their eyes closed. He reckoned they were near to death. But suddenly their eyelids lifted and the flare of recognition showed in their faces.

It was the reverend who spoke, his voice little more than a whisper. 'Thank God you've come . . . I guess the Lord

40

must have sent you.'

Ironside laughed. 'The Lord cares nothing for you,' he said. With all his whiskey gone, he was at his meanest.

'Cut us free,' Haycox pleaded.

Ironside drew the knife from his belt. 'I have some horsemeat to slice,' he said. 'Then I must be on my way. I've wasted too much time already.'

'Cut us free,' Haycox repeated, his voice desperate.

Ironside grunted with impatience and was turning away when the reverend cried out: 'If you won't release us, shift these rocks from under our backs. At least let us die in peace.'

Ironside shook his head. 'I never asked you to come on this hunt. For all I care you can rot in hell!' With that, he left them, went to the horse carcass and sliced off a ration of flesh. He then sought out his big sorrel, leaped onto its back and rode off.

The reverend started to whisper prayers, pleading with the Lord for sweet death so that they could pass through the gateway to immortality.

Haycox gazed up into the brassy sky, saw two buzzards wheeling in tireless circles as they descended. Perhaps they sensed that their patience was about to be rewarded. Haycox closed his eyes, shuddering with the venomous hatred he felt for Jason Ironside.

4

Duncan was dizzy with the pain in his leg, but he felt a desperate urge to discover what had become of Haycox and Cooper. He cherished a hope that they had somehow survived. He found a twisted stump of a mesquite branch and used it as a crutch as he attempted to return to the point where the ambush had taken place. He was hobbling slowly along when he heard the crack of gunfire . . . a number of shots fired in quick succession, followed by a pause, then two more shots — all coming from a fair way off.

He felt sure the fire had come from a handgun, and this puzzled him. He was pretty certain that the Indians had not had pistols but had relied on their bows. Who, then, had done the firing? Hope surged in him that it had been Haycox, and that he had somehow driven off the attackers.

He slumped down, trying to reason out his best course of action. He didn't want to blunder into a trap. He felt utterly weary from loss of blood and his exertions, but he'd decided to get closer to the source of the gunfire when he became aware of pounding hoofs. He saw movement a hundred yards off; a racing horseman galloping from right to left, and recognition dawned on him. It was Ironside. For a second he debated whether he should cry out and attempt to attract the man's attention — but then he recalled the throat-slit body of Fred Haycox, and the fact that Ironside had callously walked out on the party, and he remained unseen. Soon Ironside had passed from view.

Duncan suspected that Ironside had been responsible for the gunshots. Using the crutch, he managed to stand up and, moving slowly, he dragged himself through the cactus, striving to recall the direction from which the shots had sounded.

★　　★　　★

Haycox could move his arms . . . then his legs . . . and his back was no longer punished by the rock; it had been removed. But his whole body throbbed with pain. He could hear the deep tones of the reverend's voice, then another voice. It was Duncan's! He groaned. Was this part of his nightmare? Or was he dead?

'Drink this. It'll do you good.' Duncan was holding a horn of water to his lips. Haycox allowed water to seep into his mouth. He swallowed, coughed and swallowed some more. His vision was returning. He could see Duncan stooping over him and the reverend was standing behind him. Duncan helped him to sit up.

The reverend said, 'This time the Lord has truly answered our prayers. We must thank Him for our salvation.'

Haycox reached out, gripped Duncan's arm to confirm that he wasn't dreaming. Gradually he convinced himself that what he was experiencing was real. Duncan had rescued them from their terrible ordeal.

Both Haycox and Cooper were still suffering greatly; although the reverend appeared the stronger of the two, for he was standing. Duncan, too, was severely discomforted. He had been nigh spent when he had eventually hobbled into the campsite and discovered the bloody remains of the Indians who Ironside had gunned down. But he'd had an even bigger shock when he'd come upon the spread-eagled, naked bodies of Haycox and Cooper. At first he'd feared they too were dead, but then he'd seen signs of life and had breathed a sigh of relief. Renewed energy surged through his veins. He'd soon cut them free. He'd found horns of water which the Indians had left and they all drank. He also found the three hobbled horses which grazed on the stretch of grass. Close by was the half-butchered carcass of the slaughtered animal.

Over the next hours the three men

rested at a spot well away from the dead Indians. None of them had the strength to dig graves. The backs of Haycox and the reverend had been rubbed raw by the rocks; their bodies were stiff and racked with pain from the prolonged stretching; their skins were red and blistered with sunburn. But the miracle of their escape gave them a joyousness which not even their suffering could suppress. They recovered their clothing which the Indians had cast to one side and pulled it back on. Haycox also found his gunbelt and weapon.

Despite his own affliction, the reverend showed concern at Duncan's injury.

Duncan removed his bloodstained Levis to expose the wound. Cooper gently cleansed it and then, using a patch of torn-off shirt, bandaged it. But he did not like what he had seen, sensing that the wound was infected.

'You need a doctor,' he said as Duncan gingerly pulled on his Levis. 'That infection might spread.' He winced as his own pain caused a spasm.

'I guess there's no doc around here,' Duncan observed.

'Ironside mentioned a town called Pinto to the south,' Cooper said. 'Maybe it would be best to head there. He reckoned Vance and Catherine might have gone there.'

Duncan nodded. 'I guess Ironside was bluffing. I've heard of Pinto. Ironside probably wanted us to head there on a wild-goose chase while he tracked down Vance himself.'

'That may be true, but it doesn't alter the fact that you need a doctor. I'm sure there's one in Pinto. Unless you get medical attention, you could lose the leg.'

Duncan sighed with exasperation.

Amazingly the reverend expressed regret that the Indians had lost their lives.

'How can you be sorry for the devils after what they did to us?' Haycox exclaimed.

Cooper spoke in an incredibly calm

48

voice. 'When he was being crucified, Jesus said, 'Father, forgive them; for they know not what they do.' I have made the same plea.'

Duncan asked, 'So you don't hate the Indians?'

'No,' the reverend responded. 'They're all God's children.'

The other two looked at him, astounded.

Despite Cooper's compassion, Duncan feared that there might be more Indians in the vicinity. If they came upon them and discovered their dead brothers, their vengeance would be swift. However, the three of them were in no condition to travel on right now. They would have to spend at least one night at this place.

Duncan went to the horse carcass, fanned away the flies, and sliced off some flesh, noting that he was not the first to do so. Presently, they got a small fire going, roasted the meat and satisfied their hunger.

Later, they lay back, wrapped in the

blankets that the Indians had possessed. They were greasy, flea-ridden and smelled of stale sweat, but they provided warmth. Whilst the days in the desert were blisteringly hot, the nights were cold. Haycox was groaning softly, but the reverend began to snore. It was incredible that he could slumber after the ordeal he had been through. The man was amazing.

Duncan was kept awake by the squawk of buzzards, some twenty yards away, squabbling over their hierarchical place as their beaks sought the fleshy parts of the corpses. The smell of the dead permeated the air. His leg throbbed with pain. He didn't want to lose it and he wondered if the infection was spreading. Maybe he should try and reach the doctor in Pinto, but the thought of this grieved him because he was loath to give up their hunt and leave Ironside to satisfy his own motives. He reckoned that Ironside had a better idea of the whereabouts of Vance and the girl than he had let on.

But perhaps Duncan had no choice. He would have to make the final decision in the morning. Of course he couldn't expect his two companions to accompany him to Pinto. Haycox was still seething with hatred of Ironside and the craving for vengeance — and the reverend seemed determined to save lives in a situation threatening violence and death. They might well choose to continue the hunt. With his mind twisting and unsure, he lay awake for hours, seeking to relieve his pain by cursing, over and over. Eventually he slept.

Dawn's light was sifting through the overhead branches when he attempted to move. A monstrous bolt of agony slammed upwards from his leg, causing him to shout. His hands were trembling as he lowered his Levis and saw how the wound had swollen up, how it had turned green and was seeping pus.

The reverend had already risen from his blanket; his eyes were shining, there was a look of exultation on his face, and he was breathing heavily. 'Duncan,' he cried, 'the Lord has spoken to me. He told me that your wound is bad, that you will die unless action is taken straight away . . . very drastic action. There is no time to go to Pinto. With every passing minute, your life is ebbing away. He has tasked me with saving you.' He was holding a big knife that had belonged to the Indians.

My God, Duncan thought. *He means to cut my leg off!*

5

Catherine Hennessey thought she would die soon. She had vomited until her stomach churned with emptiness. Her entire body ached, including a pounding headache. During the past days she had become tired of the blistering landscape of red stone and blue sky. The heat and sparse diet left her feeling weak. What she'd considered the last straw had come earlier when they'd stopped at a water hole marked by a single cottonwood tree. She'd been afraid of the large dragonflies that hovered about her head. From the pool she'd taken a cup of water and swallowed it down. It was then that Joe Vance had shouted: '*Catherine, don't drink that. Spit it out!*'

But it was too late.

Peering into the pool and seeing what he had seen, she screamed with revulsion. Submerged in the water was the decomposing carcass of a horse; it had split open and was crusted with what looked like horseshoe crabs with poppy-seed eyes and pronged tails.

Vance was frantic with concern as he realized that the well had been poisoned by somebody who did not welcome strangers traversing the desert — possibly Indians or bandits. Despite bringing up most of what her stomach contained, Catherine was convinced that she had been poisoned.

'It was your fault,' she gasped. 'Why didn't you check before you let me drink!'

'Honey, I'm downright sorry,' he said.

Afterwards, they had travelled on until her stomach cramps became unbearable and she had fallen from her saddle onto the ground. He had dismounted immediately and cradled her shuddering body in his arms, trying to calm her and assure her that she would feel better soon. She did not believe him. She closed her eyes and held her breath. She lay still and he cried out with anguish, believing that she'd passed away. When she started to breathe again relief surged through him.

Since their elopement, things had not gone well. Before, when he'd told her about the gold mine he'd discovered, she'd expressed delight at the prospect of finding wealth and escaping from her father. She hated her father's overbearing, arrogant manner. She would be glad to hurt him in any way she could. Vance had warned her that the journey across the desert would be hard, but she'd dismissed his warnings, saying, 'I'm not a child.'

Soon, however, he realized that bringing her into this desolate place was a grave mistake. She had been used to sophisticated life in Baltimore, and she had been spoilt by her mother when she had returned to the West. Mrs Hennessey felt justified in pampering her daughters to make up for their father's bullying ways. Now, Catherine had found that living in the desert had been worse than her most awful nightmares, worse even than living at home. On the very first morning, she'd awakened to find a giant mesquite bug ambling up on her blanket towards her face, and she screamed until Vance came and brushed it off.

No matter how desperately he had tried to comfort her, to assure her that things would improve when they reached the mine, she had become increasingly distraught.

The trouble was he loved her, was besotted by her, and had been since first setting eyes on her. She was the most beautiful woman he had ever known; not even the burning sun and wearying travel could change that, and he longed to restore the glow of happiness which she'd displayed when they'd first met.

Now he gently lifted her in his arms and rested her down in a shaded spot. He fetched a blanket from his horse and fashioned a pillow which he placed beneath her head. He cursed himself for not checking the well before she'd drunk. Would she ever forgive him?

Joe Vance was thirty years old, diminutive but wiry in stature, and he had spent most of his life at odds with the law. With his mother dead and his father gone away, the then three-year-old had been kidnapped by river pirates and adopted by them.

He grew up greatly influenced by the man who became his stepfather, Jose Vance, and his stepbrother Will Vance, and he became adept at river piracy. When he was nineteen he struck out on his own, robbing stagecoaches and banks. He evaded the authorities, choosing to hide out mostly in the desert. He had a cheery disposition and prided himself that he had never killed anybody, and that he had robbed only those who could afford it, often having a joke with his victims. But in due course he had been blamed for killings and crimes he had not committed, and his name had found its way onto the 'wanted' list.

He had always yearned to trace his true father, and one day he learned that he lived in Barn Springs. He contacted him and they had a joyful reunion. However his father was very concerned about his son's occupation.

When Vance left his father's home he was crossing the nearby range when he saw a girl on a runaway horse. Racing to her aid, he eventually calmed the animal and for the first time encountered Catherine Hennessey. She had shiny, raven hair, a complexion creamy beyond belief, sensuous lips and china-blue, kittenish eyes. Soon he was head over heels in love with her. She became the single most important fact of his life.

Although risking his neck, Vance remained in the area and they met secretly and frequently. He'd told her about the gold mine he'd discovered in the mountains at the southern fringe of the desert and she had begged him to help her elope. He was only too willing. She'd seen him as the answer to all her longings for escape. Their first kiss had stirred in him overwhelming passion.

She'd confided in no one apart from her sister Rebecca. Rebecca had pleaded with her sister to allow her to accompany her; she hated their father as much as Catherine. But Catherine had refused to countenance it.

When Catherine had been at Baltimore she'd frequently been escorted by James Swarthout, who was besotted by her beauty. James was the son of Senator Theodore Swarthout who, it was said, had the ear of President Grant. However, Catherine had little regard for James, mainly because he was as fickle as she was, although she would not have realized it. Nonetheless she was happy enough to be taken to theatres and the ice rink. Since she had returned home, her father had corresponded with the senator; both expressed the wish that their offspring should become man and wife. Edward had seen a future full of promise if his daughter married into such an influential family.

When Edward Hennessey discovered that his daughter had absconded, he'd turned crimson with rage, and his wife wondered if he was succumbing to another heart attack. Catherine's elopement with a criminal would bring disgrace on his family's reputation, spoiling his ambitions of running for state governor . . . and maybe for president one day.

⋆　⋆　⋆

It was four years since Jason Ironside had made what he considered to be the greatest mistake of his life. In his duties as official hangman of Barn Springs he paid considerable attention to his rope, rubbing oil into the fibres by hand, checking its strength. He fashioned the loop and knot with its thirteen coils. The mayor of Barn Springs no longer tolerated public hangings, feeling it in bad taste. The deed was carried out in a large barn on the edge of town, usually at dawn. Ironside was paid a hundred dollars for each job, but out of that he had to buy a suit of clothes, a blanket and a coffin for the condemned man. The balance he usually gambled and drank away in the saloon.

With the usual pleasure, he had prepared for the execution of a thirty-five-year-old gambler called Chad Brimmer. Brimmer had been found guilty on two counts of murder. Having been jilted by his long-time girlfriend for another man, he killed them both in a fit of jealousy. There were witnesses of the shooting and he had no defence. The death sentence was a formality.

As was his custom, Ironside visited the condemned man in his cell on the eve of his hanging. He was slightly drunk at the time. The knowledge that he had the ability to terminate life always filled him with a powerful exultation and he delighted when his intended victim broke down, pleading for mercy, a plea that he had always scorned.

But with Brimmer the occasion was different. The man certainly begged to be spared, dropping to his knees, gripping Ironside's long black coat. Ironside was about to kick him aside, when the condemned man came out with an amazing statement.

'If you let me live, if you doctor the rope so I'm spared, I'll make you richer than you ever dreamed of. I'll swear it on the Bible if you want.'

'All murderers say that when they see their number's up,' Ironside said callously. 'I ain't got the time to listen to your lies.'

Brimmer was not put off. 'It's God's truth, I swear it. If you let me live, I'll take you to the finest gold mine ever. You can chop the gold out with an axe. An old Indian told me about it, showed me the way to it. He's dead now. You can register it in your name, have it for yourself, I promise. You'll be richer than you ever dreamed possible.'

Ironside's disbelief had melted slightly. 'Where is this so-called gold mine?' he asked.

'In the desert, in a high ridge of rock, near a water hole.'

'You got a map to prove it?'

Brimmer said, 'No. I carry the secret in my head. I called it the Rattlesnake Mine 'cos there's snakes in it. Nobody else knows about it.'

'And you'd take me there?' Ironside asked. Brimmer's revelation had sobered him up.

'I swear I would. If I live, I'll lead you across the desert. You'd never find it by yourself.'

Ironside sat down on the cell's bunk. He thought for a long moment. Eventually he asked, 'You say I have to let you survive the hanging . . . how am I gonna do that?'

Brimmer's face brightened. The words tumbled out of him. 'Just make the rope long enough for me to hit the ground. Maybe I'll break my leg, but that don't matter. Better than a broken neck.

They're bound to reprieve me after surviving the hanging, same as they did for that fella Cyrus Makepiece in Arizona. They'll change my sentence to jail. But I'll get out of jail somehow. Maybe you could help me . . . that's if you wanna be a rich man.'

Brimmer steepled his hands before him as if in prayer, his eyes pleading with Ironside.

Ironside emitted a thoughtful sigh. 'I'll think about it,' he said.

'When'll you let me know?'

Ironside stood up. 'You'll know after the trap drops away under your feet.'

That night Ironside didn't go to bed but sat up drinking whiskey; his mind was mulling over what Brimmer had told him. If he did what the man suggested, he would have some explaining to do to the mayor and town council. Maybe he wouldn't give them the chance to question him. Maybe he'd just fade away for a while, disappear. He enjoyed stretching men's necks, but the prospect of finding riches beyond his wildest dreams held great appeal. He'd always boasted that he'd never hanged a man who came back to commit more crime. But now might be the time for that to change.

Presently he set about lengthening his rope.

6

Next morning there was early activity in the Town Marshal's office as Chad Brimmer was roused from his bunk, offered a breakfast which he declined, and then handcuffed. Thirty minutes later he was led up the street, surrounded by guards, to the grim barn on the edge of town. Inside was the ugly scaffold. It loomed like a giant monster. He gazed up at the platform and saw the lever that would cause it to collapse. Waiting alongside was Ironside who gave Brimmer a nod of acknowledgement. Brimmer gazed at him, hoping for some indication as to the action he would take, but Ironside had turned away. He appeared to be swaying slightly on his feet. A number of local dignitaries were present, including the church minister Enoch Cooper.

Brimmer was given no time to

ponder. He was hastened up the scaffold steps onto the platform. The minister intoned a brief prayer for the soul of a man about to die and made the sign of the cross, then Ironside came forward and slipped a black hood over Brimmer's head. Brimmer smelt the liquor on his breath. He felt the noose being fitted around his neck; the knot under his left ear. The rope felt heavy and stiff. Ironside's rough hands adjusted it to fit properly. Brimmer's bowels rumbled. He strained his ears, praying for some whisper that would assure him that all would be well, but Ironside murmured nothing. He heard his footsteps creaking the boards as he moved back to his appointed position.

A sharp instruction rang out from below and Ironside hauled back on the lever. The platform collapsed with a ground-shaking thump; Brimmer plummeted like a stone. He knew little about it. His neck snapped and his feet dangled some six inches from the ground.

Ironside snarled with dismay. He unleashed an obscenity. He must have miscalculated the measurements. *Why the hell hadn't he stayed sober!*

After the corpse was freed from the rope, a doctor carried out an examination and certified death. Ironside climbed down from the scaffold on unsteady legs. He was choking with fury. He reckoned he'd just thrown away a fortune. The mayor stepped towards him, his hand extended. 'A good job well done,' he said.

* * *

Over the following weeks, Ironside's wrath did not diminish; in fact it increased. Eventually he reached a decision. He would conduct his own search for the Rattlesnake Mine. Accordingly, he resigned his responsibilities in Barn Springs.

For the next year he roamed the desert, crisscrossing it many times, seeking the elusive high ridge of rock which Brimmer had described. He couldn't find it, but he became familiar with the desert, familiar with the locations of the water holes. He even wandered into the villages of friendly Indians and enquired if anybody knew of the mine. Always the answer was in the negative.

At last he went back to Barn Springs, frustrated and dispirited. His drinking became heavier, his temper vitriolic. For a time he scratched a living as the town's undertaker but in due course he turned his hand to bounty hunting and managed to bring a horse thief to justice. But the reward was puny and always in his mind were thoughts of the fortune he'd missed out on. Then, in the late spring of 1873, it seemed that his luck changed.

By this time Catherine Hennessey had returned from Baltimore; she had embarked upon her affair with Joe Vance and made plans to elope. All was meant to be a secret, but Catherine was so excited at the prospect of escaping from her father that she felt the need to confide in her sister. Rebecca, disappointed that her sister had refused to allow her to accompany her, had mentioned the details to Mabel Straker who ran the general store in Barn Springs. Mrs Straker was a motherly figure and long-time friend of the girls. She was also the town's worst gossip. One day she was serving an acquaintance in the store and before she had time to shackle her tongue, she had mentioned Catherine's plans to run away with Joe Vance to his gold mine in the desert. Ironside, entering the store at that moment, heard the tail end of the conversation. It was enough to cause him to emit a half-subdued groan of excitement. The ladies paused in their chatter and looked at him in surprise. He coughed, turned away to examine some shirts on display. His heart was hammering in his chest.

A week later, Catherine was gone and Edward Hennessey offered the reward to anyone who brought her back.

Ironside seized his chance. However, he was annoyed when he learned that others were to join him in the hunt. He had no intention of leading them to the mine. He consoled himself with the thought that he could ditch them once they were in the desert.

★　★　★

Now, Catherine was lying on the mattress of blankets that Vance had fashioned for her. He'd also fixed his poncho across mesquite sticks to provide shade. She did not appreciate his care, for she was sick of the desert. Flies buzzed about her head and she felt too weak to fan them away. Furthermore, she was ill, and had suffered a fever. The sun's heat was suffocating; she could scarcely breathe. Vance had left her two hours ago to search for food, but she was sure that if she tried to eat anything she would vomit.

She dozed off and it seemed almost immediately that she was drinking from the poisoned water hole again and, to her horror, she swallowed one of the hermit crabs with its poppy-seed eyes and pronged tail. She felt it struggling as it went down her gullet, and soon it was threshing around in her stomach. It felt huge. She awoke with a scream, choking, convinced everything was real. She poked two fingers into her mouth and tried to bring the creature up . . . and then, gradually, she realized it was just a dream. She wondered if she was going mad. She lay back, panting and wretched.

Her hand touched the pistol he had left her. 'Just in case some wild creature comes a'visiting,' he'd told her. He had no idea what her true feelings were. She slipped her finger inside the guard, touched the trigger. She could end her nightmare right now if she chose. She hoped her father would grieve for her, sickened to the core that he'd mal-treated her.

* * *

Ironside was satisfied that his plans were falling into place. He had disposed of his unwanted company, he had recovered his horse and he'd wiped out a pack of troublesome Indians. Furthermore, if fortune favoured him, he would earn the reward, not only for the girl, but for Vance as well. And then, of course, there would be the Rattlesnake Mine and its haul of untapped treasure. He was counting on Vance and the girl showing him the way. He was sure that they would have followed the line of water holes, perhaps branching off when they neared their objective. Sooner or later, he reckoned, he would pick up some evidence of their passing.

That evidence came sooner than he had anticipated. A shot cracked out.

Startled by the sound, Ironside ground-tethered his horse, cocked his rifle and crept forward on foot. An uncanny instinct warned him that he was close to the man he sought. Excitement was pumping through his veins. He debated whether he should kill Vance straight away, but rejected that idea. He might never find the gold mine without him. Maybe he would just wound him.

He saw the two horses hobbled, then he came upon the makeshift shelter quite unexpectedly. The girl was lying on blankets, her arm trailing to the side. He grunted with surprise. She looked dead. Glancing around, he cautiously edged towards her. That was when he saw the rise and fall of her bosom. She was sleeping.

He wondered where Vance was. The shot he'd heard . . . maybe Vance was away hunting . . . but for how long?

Ironside glanced around, carried out a brief search, then he listened for any sound that might indicate Vance's return. He debated whether he would conceal himself in the surrounding brush and shoot the outlaw when he reappeared. He would aim for his legs and cripple him.

But his plans were to no avail because when his attention swung back to the girl, he was amazed to see her sitting up. She was gripping a pistol two-handed, and it was pointed directly at him. Her eyes blazed hatred, and for a long moment he feared she might press the trigger. She didn't. The gun was lowered. All at once a change swept over her; her expression softened and she said, 'Mr Ironside. What are you doing here?'

He forced himself to relax. 'Miss Hennessey,' he said. 'I've come to rescue you.'

'Rescue me?' she said.

'Sure,' he said.

'You'd take me out of this hell-hole of a desert?'

He nodded emphatically.

'I can't go home,' she said. 'My father would kill me . . . '

He said, 'I'll take you to some other place. Maybe to Pinto. You can start afresh there.'

She pondered on his words. She was desperate to escape the desert. She had already concluded that she didn't give a fig about Joe Vance and his uncouth manners. Any affection she'd felt for him had drained away. So, now, had her feelings of illness and helplessness. She didn't know Jason Ironside very well. She'd only met him a few times in Barn Springs, but now she made up her mind quickly. She'd grab at what he was offering. She dropped the pistol. She scrambled up from her makeshift bed.

'Get me out of this place,' she said, 'and I'll make sure you never regret it.'

He gave her one of his rare smiles. 'We must move quickly,' he said.

★   ★   ★

Earlier, Joe Vance had flushed a jackrabbit from the brush and seen the white flash of its sides as it bounded away, antelope-like, in enormous leaps. He aimed his rifle with haste and fired, sending the animal somersaulting before coming to rest. He grunted with gratification, thinking that neither Catherine nor he need go without supper tonight. Stepping forward, he picked up the rabbit by its long ears.

He decided to remain where he was for a while. Maybe he could make another kill. He'd left Catherine alone for longer than he'd intended but he figured further rest would do her no harm. He was worried about her illness. They'd been obliged to stop and rest up frequently. Their progress had been painfully slow. He lacked experience in dealing with women, apart from the soiled doves he'd fallen across. Furthermore, Catherine had been cool towards him of late, but he hoped that when she had a good supper inside her and they could push on towards the mine, she'd warm to him again.

7

The reverend had asked Haycox to rekindle the fire and to get it glowing. As the young man got to work, he glanced at Cooper and noticed the knife he was holding, also the scrap of bandage he had ripped from his own shirt and washed. Haycox then glanced across to where Duncan was lying. He seemed to have lapsed into a sort of coma.

'What are you gonna do?' Haycox gasped. 'You ain't gonna cut his leg off?'

'Not even the Lord could give me the skills for that,' the reverend said. 'All I can do is try to clean away the infected flesh. I have prayed for strength.'

Haycox nodded with relief. Even so, he felt decidedly sick. Soon the embers of the fire were glowing and the reverend pushed the knife-blade into the reddest part. 'I need to burn away any dirt,' he said. 'It's got to be clean for this job.'

Haycox stood up. His legs felt weak. He walked off, turned his back on what was happening and vomited. Not for the first time, he reckoned that the reverend had several times the amount of courage that he possessed. To his dismay, Cooper called to him.

'I need your help, Dave.'

Haycox turned and on tremulous legs joined the reverend, who said, 'I want you to hold him down while I do the cutting.'

Duncan returned to his senses abruptly. He sat up, alarm running through him. The reverend was standing over him. 'Take your Levis off,' he said.

'No, I — '

'Take them off, quick!'

With insistent hands, the reverend helped Duncan unbuckle his belt and slip out of his Levis, exposing the festering wound in his thigh. He handed Duncan a stick of wood. 'Bite on it,' he said. 'It'll help with the pain. I'm going to get rid of the infection.'

Duncan took the stick but he didn't put it between his teeth. 'I'd sooner die,' he groaned.

The reverend smiled. 'No you wouldn't,' he said. 'With the Lord's help, this will save your life. Now lie down.'

Duncan felt light-headed. Everything about him seemed bathed in a red haze. He clamped his teeth on to the stick and rested back; and immediately he felt the downward pressure of Haycox's hands on his shoulders. He struggled in vain. He bit hard on the stick but it didn't stop him from unleashing a cry of agony as the reverend started to cut. It was over quickly, but not before he'd fainted into oblivion.

Later, when awareness again flooded through him, it brought the throb of pain with it. He looked down, fearing that Cooper might have changed his mind and removed his leg; relief touched him. His thigh was wrapped with the improvised bandage and above it a strip of horse sinew had been drawn around as a tourniquet.

'You lost some blood,' the reverend said. 'I pray that what I've done will save the infection spreading, but you still need to see a doctor. You'll have to get to Pinto as soon as possible.'

Duncan swore, then immediately regretted it, being with a church man. 'I'm grateful for what you've done,' he said.

He suffered the next hours with fortitude, resting back on his blanket. Presently Cooper came and adjusted the tourniquet, after which he roasted some horseflesh and they fed.

'Like I told you,' the reverend said as he fingered meat into his mouth, 'you've got to go to Pinto and get proper treatment, else you might still lose that leg.'

Duncan knew he was right and was angry that Fate had dealt him such a cruel hand. 'I guess I can make it by myself,' he said.

The reverend shook his head. 'You'd fall off your horse halfway there. Dave must go with you.'

Haycox looked aggrieved. 'I wanna kill Ironside,' he said. 'I owe him that. Apart from leaving us to die, he killed my brother.'

'How d'you know?' Duncan asked. 'It could've been Indians.'

Haycox shook his head in disbelief, but the reverend said, 'That could be true.'

'Why can't you go to Pinto with Duncan?' Haycox asked. 'Or maybe all three of us could go?'

'I've got to press on,' Cooper said. 'The Lord has given me the task of saving life.'

'But you'll get lost in the desert,' Duncan said, finishing his meal. 'You'll never find Vance and the girl.'

The reverend smiled. 'The Lord will show me the way. After all, Jesus spent forty days and forty nights in the wilderness.'

Duncan reckoned it was pointless

arguing with the reverend who could be tiresome at times, figuring he had an answer for everything. But maybe this time he wouldn't live to regret his foolishness. Anyway, he couldn't be denied. He was a strong character.

Haycox was not happy about the situation and argued against accompanying Duncan for some time, but eventually conceded. They waited until the afternoon and then decided to make a move. Their present location was plagued by flies and the stench from the Indian corpses and they would be glad enough to leave.

They checked the horses. There were three shaggy mustangs, left by their now-deceased owners, and the only saddles were hide-pad ones stuffed with buffalo hair. However, these would have to do. Each man sliced some meat from the horse carcass, cutting from the inside to avoid parts which were fly-blown. By this time it was somewhat rank.

They rode together for three hours,

following game trails through mesquite. The reverend had been right. Duncan was in pain and felt dizzy with loss of blood. Twice he fell from his animal and had to be assisted back. They stopped several times to rest.

Gradually the cactus thinned and the terrain became greener, with swaths of grass and frequent water holes. Flocks of small birds were flushed from the undergrowth as the horses plodded through it, circling the riders, and then settling again. Surprisingly, they came across a gnarled fingerpost. God only knew what public-spirited individual had planted it. The sun-bleached lettering on its board was only just discernible: *Pinto 30 miles.* It was pointing to the south-west.

The reverend now shook hands with his companions and bade them god-speed. He rode away, heading due south. Duncan and Haycox watched his departure with sadness. Haycox had a tear in his eye.

'May God help him,' he murmured,

'because nobody else will.'

'I hope his faith stands him in good stead,' Duncan remarked, and wondered if they would ever see him again.

* * *

Catherine had hoped that Ironside would offer her an immediate escape from the present encampment, but she was disappointed.

'Joe will be back soon,' she said. 'He'll never agree to me going with you.'

Ironside took hold of her arm. 'Don't worry,' he said. 'We'll wait for him, but we won't let him see us. We'll hide in the mesquite.'

She gave him a bewildered look, but he pulled her to the side and forced her to hunker down beside him in the concealing shrubbery. He cautioned her to be quiet. He placed his rifle on the ground and unholstered his pistol.

'What are you going to do?' she gasped.

He whispered, 'You'll see.' He checked that his pistol was fully loaded and thumbed back the hammer.

She gazed at him with wide eyes. 'You're not going to kill Joe?'

'No . . . I'm not gonna kill him. Now don't make a sound.'

She was puzzled, but she was frightened of Ironside. His big left hand was close to her arm and she sensed that he would grab her if she made any attempt to move away. They waited, the only sound being the buzz of flies and the occasional stirring of the horses grazing in the open a little way off. Vance had been gone longer than she had expected.

But at last they heard him approaching through the mesquite and shortly he came into view, carrying the rabbit. His wait for further game had been in vain. Vance pulled up when he saw that Catherine was nowhere in sight.

He called, 'Catherine?' and Ironside held up a warning hand to ensure the girl's silence.

Vance had now turned his back on them and that was when Ironside lifted his gun and aimed at the outlaw's thigh, his intention being to disable him. But as he pulled the trigger, Catherine reached out and pushed his arm. Her lack of love for Joe, even her dislike, had not been enough to allow him to be shot. However her sudden rash deed did not have the desired effect. Ironside's bullet went higher than he'd intended, striking Vance in the back, just below his right shoulder-blade. He unleashed a scream of pain and was hurled forward, landing flat on his face.

Ironside was furious. He thrust the girl away. 'You bitch!' he snarled. 'You made me kill him.'

They both rushed forward and crouched over the outlaw's body. The bullet hole in his back showed clearly, blood oozing from it.

'I never meant to kill him,' Ironside muttered.

She was distraught, emitting long sobs. 'I'm sorry. I never . . . '

Ironside was peering at the body and realized that Vance was still breathing.

'He ain't dead,' he said. 'Let's turn him over.'

Catherine nodded, dragging her hand across her face to dry her tears. Together they rolled Vance onto his back. His eyes were clamped shut.

'He'll die,' she said.

Ironside snapped out, 'Don't say that!' But he feared she was right and he was trembling with rage. He couldn't believe what had happened. He couldn't accept that, for the second time, fate was denying him the opportunity to learn the location of the Rattlesnake Mine.

8

Duncan and Haycox arrived in Pinto, which was a bustling fair-sized fishing town on the brink of the ocean. Duncan was still suffering from his wound; and also the travail of riding on an Indian saddle over rough ground had taken its toll, and both men were weary. Haycox had remained silent, and Duncan guessed he was still grieving for his dead brother. However they appreciated their return to a civilized region. On enquiring of a passer-by, they were directed to a Doctor Malmuddy's surgery on East Street. Within minutes they had found it and hitched their horses outside. Duncan hobbled in Haycox's wake as they stepped up on the boardwalk. Haycox tugged on the bell.

The door was opened by a rotund young lady in a plain blue dress with a low-cut bodice. She had rose-red lips.

Duncan spoke up: 'I need to see the doctor. I had an arrow in my leg.'

'My word,' she said. 'You'd better come in. The doctor's away right now. I'm his wife. My name's Augustine . . . and I'm a nurse, so I guess I can help you.'

Duncan nodded, but as he stepped inside Haycox held back. 'While you're getting treated,' he said, 'I'll go and set up camp on the hill. I'll see you later.'

Duncan had the feeling that Haycox was somehow frightened of the buxom femininity that this girl exuded.

'Duncan,' she said, 'it must've been scary getting that arrow in your leg. I bet it hurt real bad.'

'It did some.' He nodded. He was sprawled on the couch in the doctor's tiny surgery. On shelves surrounding them were countless drugs, liniments, ointments, painkillers and jars of pills. They were placed so haphazardly that he had the feeling that the slightest movement might bring them crashing down.

Augustine was awfully close to him and he felt uneasy. He wished he'd not been so willing to slip out of his Levis, but she had said she was a nurse. Now he pulled his shirt-tail tight about his manhood, exposing the soiled bandage that the reverend had wrapped around his thigh. He felt her hands loosening the bandage and pulling it off. He felt embarrassingly naked. She glanced at his wound, made tutting sounds through pursed lips.

'My word,' she said. 'It sure needs bathing. I'll fetch a bowl of water and a pad.' She rose away from him and returned with the necessary items. She sat on the couch, so close he could feel the press of her body. She started to swab the dirt and congealed blood away from his thigh. Duncan gazed down, his glance settling on her hands — well-rounded, determined hands that seemed to be moving up from the wound, her fussing going far wider than he had expected. He breathed in deeply.

'You got fine, strong legs,' she whispered. She raised the side of her mouth in a wry smile. He reckoned she was pretty in a brazen, plumpish sort of a way and her thin cotton dress seemed to be fighting a losing battle in covering her ample body.

'I get lonely here,' she said. 'You see, my husband's away so much.'

'Away?' he queried.

'Sure. He's nearly always out, seeing to birthings and sick folk. And when he comes home, he's usually so tired. He thinks bed's for sleeping, nothing else.'

'He's older than you?'

She nodded. 'Sure . . . thirty years.'

Her dark hair had come loose, a wayward lock hiding half her face. He could see only one of her eyes and that was fixed on him. He could feel her hand creeping up the inside of his thigh. He shifted higher on the couch, but it didn't seem to discourage her. He reckoned he should keep her talking.

He felt no passion for her.

'How come you married him?' His words came in a rush, and she laughed.

'You ain't frightened of me, are you, Duncan?'

'No,' he said. 'I just wanted to know how come you married a man thirty years older than you.'

'I don't want to talk about him,' she murmured. 'In fact I don't want to talk at all.'

The front of her dress had somehow popped undone, displaying a plunging cleavage. She gripped his shirt-tail. He placed a restraining hand over hers.

'Your husband may come back,' he groaned.

'Not for hours.'

She withdrew her fingers from his crotch, eased herself on top of him and cupped his face in her hands. She seemed smotheringly heavy. Suddenly she covered his mouth with hers. He flinched, tried to twist away, but she was manhandling him into submission.

And then suddenly the weight of her

bore down on his injured thigh, sending a great shaft of pain, like a hot iron, shooting through him. He yelled out, thrust her aside with all his strength. She landed on the floor with a loud thump and she was howling with fury.

'You son of a bitch!' she spluttered.

It was then that they heard an outside door rattle open and the heavy footfalls of somebody entering. The doctor, home earlier than expected, entered the surgery — a heavily built, bald-headed man with bushy sideburns and whiskers; he was wearing wire-rimmed spectacles. His gaze swung from his wife and came to rest on Duncan.

'I see my wife's been attending to you,' he said.

* * *

After the Reverend Enoch Cooper had left Duncan and Haycox he'd prayed for some sign, some vision, from the heavens which would point the route he was to take — the route which would

94

lead him to Joe Vance, Catherine Hennessey and, most likely, Jason Ironside. But such enlightenment did not immediately come to him.

As he rode the Indian mustang he'd acquired, his body ached with the pummelling it had taken: the bruising, the sunburn, the discomfort caused by the lack of a white-man's saddle and stirrups, but he was a person who preferred to dwell on his fortunes rather than his misfortunes.

His mind pondered on the clear message he'd received from the Lord. It had come to him while he was tending his flock back in Barn Springs, telling him to embark on this adventure. It seemed like an aeon ago, so much had happened since. He'd seen it as the greatest challenge of his life and one he could not refuse. Now, he'd overcome many obstacles, and didn't know what lay ahead of him. But he had the confidence that faith in divine guidance brought. And perhaps such guidance was manifested in the plodding direction that his beast followed. Perhaps this was the form of the enlightenment he sought. But impatience arose in him and with it a warning that, if Ironside was somewhere ahead of him, the time he had was not limitless.

After making steady progress through the merciless heat of the afternoon, he came upon a water hole, where both he and the mustang refreshed themselves. It was as he crouched, cupping water to his mouth, that a shadow fell across him and the awesome scent of unwashed bodies and grease touched his nostrils. A tremor of fear rippled along his spine.

He rose and turned to see three Indian warriors watching him.

9

Jason Ironside was desperate. Once again his plans for tracing the mine appeared to have been thwarted. But now Ironside's interest quickened as he realized that Vance was still breathing. Suddenly his eyes opened and he gave Ironside a long, hard look. He tried to speak but couldn't make it.

Catherine was all at once overcome with compassion. Previously she'd not cared much for this man she'd eloped with, but now, seeing him gunned down had awakened an intense emotion of love in her fickle heart. The discovery that he was still alive brought tears flooding down her cheeks.

Ironside pushed her aside and stooped low over the wounded outlaw.

'You're gonna be all right,' he whispered. 'I'll get you to the doc in Pinto. He'll patch you up like new.'

Catherine could hardly believe her ears. 'Why did you shoot him?' she gasped, wiping her eyes with the back of her hand.

Ironside grunted with impatience. 'I never meant to hit him,' he lied. 'You jerked my arm, nearly made me kill him.' His voice dropped to a whisper for her ears alone. 'In fact he may still peg out if we don't get him to the doc. I'll need your help. Together, maybe we can save him. But if you act up in any way, I'll let him die. That's a promise.'

She recoiled with shock but nodded her understanding. She was afraid of Ironside, and the sudden rekindling of her love for Joe Vance made her determined not to anger the former hangman.

Ironside now focused his attention on Vance. He had closed his eyes again. Ironside decided to let him rest and consoled himself with the knowledge that while Vance survived, there was every hope of locating the mine. After that, there was no reason to keep him alive. The problem was that the outlaw was in no condition to cooperate at present, and might never be, unless a doctor could restore him to passable health.

But Vance still had a price on his head, and in taking him to Pinto Ironside would have to be careful to conceal his identity.

Catherine fussed over the sleeping Vance, wishing she could do something to revive him, but not knowing what. Her experiences in the sophisticated surroundings of Baltimore had not prepared her for these circumstances.

Meanwhile, Ironside had wandered off and recovered his own sorrel horse, which had remained ground-tethered. He'd had no fears when he'd left Catherine with Vance, being confident that she would not try to escape.

Leading his horse, he returned to the campsite and put his animal to graze with those of the outlaw and the girl. He tasked Catherine with starting a fire and skinning and cooking the rabbit.

She undertook these jobs with some disdain, particularly the skinning of the rabbit. Her fingers became bloody as she clumsily sliced at the body with a knife.

Ironside searched for lengthy branches which he bound together with rope, and it took him an hour to fashion a crude travois. Eventually he was satisfied that this would form a stretcher for Vance. They then ate their supper. Catherine tried to get the outlaw to take a little sustenance, but he refused with a shake of his head and a groan. But now his eyes were open and were fixed on Ironside.

His voice came as a weak gurgle — just one word: 'Why . . . ?'

Ironside said, 'I'm glad to see you're still in the land of the living. I guess the answer to your question is that you're a wanted man, and there's a price on your head — dead or alive.' He poked more sticks into the fire, then he went on, 'But I been thinking. I don't need to turn you in. If you cooperate I'll get you to Pinto, get you patched up by a doc, and all I ask in exchange is that you show me where the gold mine is. Seems to me that's a fair bargain?'

He glanced at Vance, but the outlaw appeared to have gone back to sleep.

Night was now coming on with its desert-swiftness. Ironside, acting like an attentive nursemaid, made Vance as comfortable as possible, hoping that he would survive the hours of darkness and the rough ride to town. He was now breathing strongly and blood was no longer seeping from his wound. A while back, Ironside would have gladly slipped a noose around this man's neck and sent him swinging to eternity. Now he desperately needed to keep him alive, at least for the present.

Turning to Catherine, he told her to bed down. They would head for Pinto in the morning.

For hours she was unable to sleep. Instead she gazed up at the moon and listened to the eerie night-calls of coyotes. She shuddered frequently. She feared that a snake or giant lizard might crawl on to her. She longed to reach Pinto. At least there would be a form of civilization there. She would then have to plan her future.

She wasn't the only one to remain awake. Ironside, lying in his blankets on the opposite side of the fire, was restless. His thoughts for once slipped away from the prospect of finding gold. Instead, he dwelt upon images of the girl's lips, breasts and loins, and his big hands clenched and unclenched as desire grew in him; his breathing became heavy. He had been without a woman for too long. Now, his lust became unbearable, bringing an animalistic growl from his throat. He restrained himself no longer. He scrambled up from his blanket and crept across to where the girl lay.

*　*　*

Malmuddy pressed the rim of a glass to Duncan's lips, forcing him to swallow a

102

bitter-tasting potion. Duncan lay back on the couch, seeing the doctor's angry expression. The man's eyes were magnified by the thick lenses of his spectacles. Grey mists were clouding Duncan's senses as Malmuddy's hard fingers probed the wound. 'The leg will have to come off,' the doctor said, 'and I'll carry out castration at the same time.'

'That'll serve him right!' Augustine's scowling face joined her husband's. They seemed to be hovering over him like galleons' figureheads appearing through the fog. Once he had thought the girl pretty, but now she appeared as a pudding-faced ogress.

It seemed much later that he drifted up through a twilight into full consciousness and he inhaled the overwhelming smell of carbolic. He was still sprawled on the couch but now a blanket covered him. He could see Malmuddy's back. He seemed to be mixing drugs, pouring liquid from one bottle to another. There was no sign of Augustine.

A horrifying thought struck Duncan.

He cast back the blanket and gazed at his thigh. It was heavily bandaged. He tentatively touched it, felt solidity beneath the bandage. He fingered his crotch and he emitted a great sigh of relief. He was still fully intact. '*Damn dream!*' he grunted.

Hearing movement, Malmuddy turned. He glared at Duncan.

'My leg,' Duncan said, anxious to break the silence, 'will it be all right?'

The doctor nodded. 'I didn't feel like fixing it, but I wasn't going to break my Hippocratic oath for a dirty rat like you. It'll heal so you're fit enough to stand trial.'

'Trial?' Duncan couldn't believe his ears.

'Sure. You'll stand trial for what you've done.'

'What have I done?' Duncan gasped.

Malmuddy said, 'Augustine told me how you raped her.'

★   ★   ★

On this rare occasion, the Reverend Cooper was lost for words. He'd been caught completely unawares. The Indians had come upon him as silently as shadows. He just gazed at them, seeing how their bodies were decorated with tattoos. They were immensely tall and their heads were shaved apart from a scalplock. Beads dangled from their ears. For the moment it seemed they were as lost for words as he was. But he thought: *They're out to avenge the deaths of their fellow warriors.* They were unlikely to heed any pleas of innocence, even from a Sunday doctor.

The foremost Indian, clearly a chief, was naked, like the others, apart from a breechclout and moccasins. He broke the silence with a flood of guttural words which brought nods of agreement from his companions. He gestured with his tomahawk towards the reverend's mustang, indicating that the white man should mount up. Cooper nodded and did as instructed, causing some mirth among the Indians for he managed it clumsily, the primitive Comanche saddle being without stirrups.

The chief grasped the reins and led him forward for some time. They passed through mesquite and cactus, the other Indians following on foot. Presently they reached the point where the party had left their own animals; the three warriors mounted up and they proceeded as a group. The reverend was given no choice but to ride along. He deeply regretted that he had been prevented from catching up with Ironside and aborting any killing he had in mind. Now, he had no idea what the future held, but experience had taught him that those unfortunate enough to be captured by Indians generally only had a torturous death awaiting them.

His companions were not talkative, but they were constantly alert, scanning far and wide whenever the terrain permitted. He sensed that any attempt at escape on his part would bring his immediate demise. As they progressed he silently prayed, putting all his trust in the Lord. He prayed that his courage would not desert him in the ordeals that lay ahead, and he chastised himself for the doubts that he'd had.

10

Catherine had not slept, or even dozed. She hated the darkness and the desert, the heat and the evil creatures that dwelt in it. She wished she was back in Baltimore. She lay in her blankets wide-eyed. Flies buzzed around her head. She wondered how much further it was to Pinto. She puzzled over what she would do on arrival. Of one thing she felt sure: she would never go near her father again. She had reached no satisfactory conclusion to her thoughts when a shadowy figure loomed over her. She screamed, brought the heavy pistol out from beneath her blanket and fired. Thank God she had kept hold of it when she'd bedded down! Its roar was thunderous, but through the reverberation she heard Ironside cursing over and over. She realized it was he who had crept up on her.

'Why the hell did you do that?' he snarled.

With the bullet passing so close that he felt its breath burn his cheek, all Ironside's lecherous desires had dissipated. He was stunned by the knowledge that, but for a waver in the girl's hand, his brain could have been blown from his head. Trembling with shock, he sprang forward and snatched the weapon from her grasp, then struck her across the side of the face with his hand.

His blow made her dizzy. Her voice came in a stutter. 'I . . . I thought you were a grizzly bear.'

He grunted with impatience. 'You could've killed me, you bitch. All I wanted was to make sure you was tucked in cosy. Now you better get to sleep before I give you a good spanking!'

He turned, went back to his own blanket and slumped down. She heard him muttering to himself.

Next morning they rose with dawn's light. Vance tried to sit up, but couldn't make it. He lay back, groaning.

After Ironside and the girl had finished the last of the rabbit, they prepared to pull out. Catherine had a huge bruise on her cheek where she'd been struck. She helped Ironside transfer Vance onto the travois and tie him with rope so he wouldn't fall off.

Having attached the travois to the big sorrel, they mounted the other horses and rode out. Mid-morning they passed the old fingerpost. Its lettering still proclaimed: *Pinto — 30 miles.*

★　★　★

The reverend was given no indication of the fate that awaited him as he rode with the Indians. The miles fell behind and darkness drifted in about them. On one occasion he dozed off but awoke suddenly, only just preventing himself from falling from his horse. He was glad his hands had not been bound. The moon had now become bright in the sky, changing the landscape to a ghostly sculpture. The desert had given way to rocky foothills. Presently they reined in, and the chief cupped his hands to his mouth, sending a wolf-call into the night, repeated twice over. The echo-like response came almost immediately, bringing grunts of satisfaction from the others. Fifteen minutes later they rode up a narrow ravine and reached a small encampment where a low fire glimmered and a single tepee was pitched.

The arrival brought a welcoming excitement from the half-dozen Indians who were in the camp. They grew silent as the chief gestured towards the reverend and launched into a lengthy speech. Cooper realized he was the centre of attention. When the chief finished, he indicated to the reverend that he was to dismount. This he did and was so stiff that he almost fell over.

A very strange thing happened. The chief, now also afoot, extended his hand. Cooper suspected that he might become the victim of a trap, but being a trusting man, he reached out his own hand and, to his surprise, it was grasped in a long shake by the Indian. The gesture was greeted with ebullient murmurings from all around.

A young woman appeared at his side. He could not see her clearly in the darkness but he did glimpse her slim figure and the glint of her teeth and knew she was smiling.

'You are a Sunday doctor?' she asked in perfect English.

'Yes,' he nodded. 'I preach the word of the Lord God. Who are you, my dear?'

'I am called Always Laughing.'

'That is a lovely name,' he said. 'You speak good English.'

He heard her gentle laugh. 'I am a white girl. I was captured by the Comanche when I was eight. My parents were killed. A year later, I was traded to the Osage.'

'Then these people are not Comanche?'

Always Laughing shook her head. 'We are Wah-Zha-Zhe. The whites call us Osage. The Comanche are our enemies.'

He was aware that the interest in him had diminished. The Indians who had been watching him, including the chief, had wandered off. The appetizing aroma of food emanated from a cooking pot suspended over the fire. Another woman was tending it.

The reverend had heard of the Osage, heard how they had defeated the Kiowa in the so-called Cut Throat Massacre and after the battle had cut off the heads of the vanquished and displayed them in copper pots.

'The Osage are friendly with the whites?' he asked.

'Yes. One of our chiefs helped Yellow Hair Custer at the Battle of Washita River.' She pointed to the Indians gathering around the cooking pot. 'Now you should eat.'

He was more than willing to comply and soon he was sitting with his hosts, having been given a bowl hollowed out of a cottonwood knot and filled with an assortment of squash, nuts and berries. He was comforted, for he had heard that the Osage only ate meat when they were intent on war. He ate with his fingers and had never appreciated food more. Both the chief and Always Laughing sat close to him. The chief conferred with the girl at length. She then turned to the reverend and said, 'Big Horse asks: why were you travelling in this country?'

He wiped his bowl clean with his fingers and licked them. He saw no point in concealing the truth. 'I am searching for a gold mine.'

Always Laughing suddenly stiffened. She passed the information on to Big Horse who nodded sagely. She turned back to the reverend. 'Why are you searching?' she asked.

'Because I believe that men will be there who wish to fight,' he explained. 'I want to prevent the killing if I can.'

'Why?'

'I have been sent by God to save life,' he said.

She nodded as if everything was clear, then said, 'The place is evil, full of rattlesnakes.'

He nodded. 'You have been there?'

'Joe took me there — '

'Joe?' he cut in excitedly.

'Joe Vance,' she said. 'He stayed in our camp for a while. He had stepped on a horned toad and he got sick. I nursed him till he was well. Afterwards, he showed me the mine. I saw the streaks of gold in the rock.'

'Always Laughing,' said Cooper, 'I have a favour to ask. Will you take me to the mine?'

For a moment she was silent, then she said, 'I will take you if you will tell me about your God and about Jesus. I learned about them when I was a child, but living with the Osage I have lost the way. I wish to pray to God in heaven and hear again the stories.'

In an elated voice he said, 'I will gladly tell you, and we can pray together.'

She laughed happily. 'Then I will

115

take you to the mine,' she said, 'but not yet. I am nursing the old mother of Big Horse. I cannot leave her until she is better.'

The reverend nodded. He regretted the delay but he had no option.

11

Catherine was in a back room of the guest house into which Ironside had booked them. She was absent-mindedly prodding the coloured balls about on a green-baized pool table. James Swarthout had introduced her to the game when she had been in Baltimore. But she was not concentrating on it because she was alone and, more important, her thoughts were on other matters.

Ironside had left her an hour ago, having gone back to the surgery where he'd left Joe Vance in the care of Doctor Malmuddy. He had told her to remain in the guest house. But she was tired of being bossed around by the overbearing Ironside and now, inwardly, she was pondering on what her options were for the future. She had no wish to remain with the ex-hangman, and she found that the feelings she had for Joe Vance had, once again, flowed away.

The journey to Pinto had been tiresome and the outlaw, borne on the travois, had been weak and had remained in a semi-conscious state. She had concluded that he would never be the lover for whom she yearned. Clearly the doctor was unaware of the outlaw's identity and Ironside would do his utmost to ensure that his presence would not be advertized.

Now that Vance was in the hands of a physician Catherine no longer felt any responsibility towards him. But there was one aspect about him that drew her thoughts — the fact that a substantial reward had been offered for his apprehension.

She had little money of her own, and if she was to carve out a future for herself the reward for reporting the outlaw's presence to the local marshal would be most welcome. She consoled herself with the belief that Vance would be cared for at some prison hospital, so that his recovery would not be compromised. Of course Ironside would be livid, for he was intent on using the outlaw to guide him to the gold. But, if fortune smiled, she would be long gone before he could catch her.

The plan took root in her mind. Shortly, she went out in search of the marshal's office.

★ ★ ★

That evening Haycox had left Duncan at the camp they'd made on the hill overlooking the town and ventured into the saloon on Main Street. The place was thronging with fishermen who were celebrating a big catch, and beer in foaming tankards was flowing freely. Fancy-dressed girls were soliciting for custom. Several card tables were operating and a woman, accompanied by a piano, was striving to make herself heard as she sang 'Little Brown Jug'; her voice sounded as if she was gargling with axle grease.

Haycox elbowed his way to the bar and set himself up with a beer. Despite the surrounding joviality, depression at the loss of his brother still plagued him.

He was taking his first sip of liquor when he turned and came face to face with Ironside. Both men's jaws dropped as recognition struck them.

'Thought you was dead . . . ' Ironside gasped, his eyes suddenly as cold as the eyes of a lynx, the muscles playing along his jaw.

'Just like my brother, you murderous bastard!' Haycox spat out; then he lunged at the big man, catching him a blow on his rock-hard chin.

Amid shouts and screams, Ironside grabbed a half-full bottle and smashed it against the bar-top, spewing whiskey all around. He then jabbed the jagged glass at Haycox's face, but the younger man dodged aside. He swung a great haymaking punch at Ironside but missed by a mile. Snarling with rage, Ironside launched a further thrust of the shattered bottle, this time catching

Haycox on the cheek, bringing forth a gush of blood.

Meanwhile there'd been a drawing back of the crowding drinkers as they sought both safety and a place from which to spectate. Shouts and screams subsided. The sudden hush was broken only by the grunts and snarls of the two fighters.

Ironside, a foot taller, towered over Haycox. Somehow he had cut his own hand on the bottle; the resultant blood caused it to slip from his grasp. Undaunted, he sprang at Haycox like a pouncing cougar, his great hands reaching for the small man's throat. Haycox, swifter on his feet, danced to the side, then slammed his boot into Ironside's groin. Ironside cried out with sudden pain, but the hurt fuelled his rage. Again, he jumped at Haycox, this time getting his arms around him, crushing him in a powerful bear-hug. The two men were stilled for a moment, Haycox helpless in the deadly embrace as he strove to breathe, then they both toppled over, crashing to the sawdusted floor, Ironside's considerable weight on top.

Haycox lay smothered, knowing he was flattened and beaten. His lungs felt that they were collapsing. His senses became blurred, pierced by somebody shouting: 'He's gonna kill him!'

'*Hold on!*' A stentorian voice cut through the general burble and heads turned to see a thickset man with a badge pinned to his blue flannel shirt stepping into the saloon. He had long, greying hair down to his shoulders. Somebody mouthed his name: *Marshal Clayburn,* and the throng drew back, respectfully creating a pathway for the man who had maintained law in the town for the last ten years.

Ironside, his face gleaming with sweat, looked up and immediately he rolled clear of Haycox and came to his feet. He met the lawman's steely gaze.

'He tried to kill me,' he said.

Haycox was sitting up, drawing air

into his lungs in great gasps. His face was ashen.

'Looks like he nigh got hisself killed,' the marshal remarked.

From behind him somebody spoke: 'Yeah, that little fella sure struck the first blow.'

'I was just defending myself,' Ironside explained, licking blood from his fist.

Haycox was still struggling with his breathing. He stood up, swaying on his feet. 'He killed my brother,' he mumbled but Clayburn seemed not to hear.

The lawman drew his gun and said, 'I'm taking him in. He'll have some explaining to do in the morning when he sobers up.'

'I ain't drunk!' Haycox exclaimed.

The marshal said, 'Hand over your gun, mister.'

Haycox hesitated, then grudgingly complied with the order.

Ten minutes later he was locked in a cell.

★ ★ ★

At first, Augustine Malmuddy had acted contritely after she'd explained to her husband how the man called Duncan had callously raped her. Now, in the practice's small infirmary, she made her patient comfortable in bed and watched over him while he dozed off. Still drowsy from the laudanum administered while the doctor had extracted the bullet, Vance was soon snoring softly.

Augustine relaxed in her chair. She was still smarting over the way Duncan had rejected her advances, and still annoyed by the early return of her husband. Now, her eyes rested on the recumbent form of Vance and she wondered if he would enjoy being pleasured by her. Presently she heard the outside bell ring; she rose and passed through the surgery to the front door. Opening up, she was confronted by the tall figure of Ironside.

'I've come to visit the patient,' he announced.

'He's asleep right now,' she said.

'Oh, he'll wake up when he hears what I've got to tell him.'

'Oh well, come in,' she said.

He followed her as she led the way back to the infirmary. To her surprise, her patient was already awake, but he didn't show any pleasure as the visitor entered.

Ironside turned to the woman and said, 'Can you leave us alone for a minute? I have something confidential to discuss.'

Augustine hesitated. 'Well, he's still groggy from the laudanum.'

'I won't keep him long,' Ironside said.

She nodded and departed. But she went no further than the other side of the door. Inquisitiveness took hold of her and she strained her ears to catch what was said. Ironside's words carried clearly.

'Now listen here. I could turn you over to the law if I wanted, but, like I said before when you pretended not to hear, I'm willing to strike a bargain. As soon as you're fit enough to fork a horse, you lead me to the gold mine and we'll go into partnership, go fifty-fifty on what we make. If you don't agree, then you'll go to jail; that's a promise.'

Vance emitted a long sigh, then said, 'I guess I got no choice.' Then he asked, 'Where's Catherine? Is she all right?'

'She's over at the guest house, resting. She's fine.'

Augustine was excited by what she'd heard. She didn't quite know why but mention of a gold mine had caused her heart to pound. She retreated to the surgery and was there when Ironside passed through, wishing her good night. He was soon gone.

* * *

At the small encampment at the edge of Pinto, Duncan slept soundly that night. When he awoke in the morning he was surprised to see that Haycox had not returned from his trip into town. He knew he wouldn't have got drunk because he'd lent him only a small sum of money.

Duncan hobbled to his horse, saddled it and mounted up. He went down into Pinto's Main Street and found the saloon. The place was empty apart from a man mopping the floor. Duncan explained that his friend was missing and, after some explanation, learned that he had been arrested by the marshal. Duncan nodded his thanks; five minutes later he found the marshal's office and entered.

Clayburn was sitting at his desk reading an old newspaper.

'I hear you arrested my friend Haycox,' Duncan said.

The marshal nodded and smiled. 'He'd got himself into a fight with a fella twice his size. I put him in the jail for his own safety as much as for anything else.'

'Then you'll let him out now?'

'I guess so,' Clayburn said. He stood up, lifted a big key from the rack behind him. Soon Haycox had been set free.

The sight of his bruised face and the ugly cut on his cheek brought a shocked gasp from Duncan.

'Ironside's in town,' Haycox explained. 'I guess we came to blows.'

'Well, you stay clear of trouble now,' the marshal advised and the young man nodded.

Clayburn gave Duncan a long stare; the pleasantness in his face drained away and was replaced by a scowl. 'You're the fella called Duncan, are you?' he asked.

'That's me.'

The marshal snatched his pistol from its holster. 'Then I'm arresting you on suspicion of rape!' he said.

* * *

The previous evening, Catherine Hennessey had left the guest house and set about finding the marshal's office. She walked furtively, frequently glancing over her shoulder. She was terrified that Ironside might suddenly appear and unleash his fury upon her. She was soon trembling violently. With darkness deepening, she walked the length of Main Street and was unable to find the establishment she sought. She asked the way from a passer-by and was directed down a side street, eventually finding the lawman's office. A light glowed from within. Picking up courage, she rang the bell and entered.

A man was sprawled on the chair, his hat pulled over his face, his feet on the desk before him. He was a small man and now he spluttered to wakefulness, pushing his hat back and lowering his feet. He was embarrassed that such a good-looking woman should call on him this late at night. She looked thoroughly agitated. 'Yes, ma'am?' he said.

'Are you the marshal?' she enquired.

'No, ma'am. He's out. He went down to the saloon. There's often trouble there. I'm his deputy. Can I help you?'

She hesitated. Visions of Ironside finding out what she was doing overwhelmed her. She felt faint. She'd been foolish to reason the way she had.

'Are you all right?' the deputy said, standing up.

'Y-yes,' she said. 'I wanted to speak to the marshal. M-maybe I'll call in tomorrow.'

She turned, left the office and hurried back along the sidewalk. She prayed that Ironside had not returned. If he had, she would have to run off into the night . . . and then what?

She reached the guest house, rushed up to her room and fell across her bed. She shuddered with relief. He had not yet come back from his visit to Joe Vance. Maybe he'd stopped at the saloon.

12

Reverend Enoch Cooper had seldom enjoyed such charming company as Always Laughing guided him towards the mine. She certainly lived up to her name, only growing serious when he related stories from the Bible. She had big brown eyes, like those of a deer. She looked pretty in her buckskin dress, decorated with porcupine quills, with leggings to match. She listened enrapt to the exploits of Daniel in the lions' den, of Samson and Goliath, of Moses leading the Israelites from Egypt, and the parting of the Red Sea. But she preferred to hear about the birth of Jesus and how he had worked miracles, sometimes clapping her hands with delight. Many of these stories she had learned as a child, but memory of them had faded as she'd become steeped in Osage culture.

She was a proper chatterbox. As they rode through treeless land, she told him how, when she was eight years old, her white family had decided to move to Santa Fe and had joined a caravan of a dozen high-wheeled wagons. They were well covered with canvas to keep out dust and rain. They left Independence and travelled west, crossing several rivers. The wagons, winding like a sluggish snake, were hauled by oxen because Indians had no use for them and would not steal them.

She remembered the final morning quite clearly because her ma told her the sky was as blue as a robin's egg. She had never seen a robin's egg. She guessed it must be very blue. They reached a long hill. The grade was too steep for oxen, and the men, who had been acting as guards, dismounted, let their horses stray to the side to crop the grass, while they grabbed the wheel-spokes of the wagons, straining hard to move up the slope. It was while they were thus exposed that the attack came.

132

The great war party of Comanches came charging down from the crest of the hill, discharging arrows as they rode and filling the air with their chilling war cries.

Always Laughing remembered how her mother had pushed her back into the wagon and covered her with a blanket, then thrown her own body on top for protection. Nigh suffocating, the girl had heard the pandemonium raging outside: the thunder of guns, the shrieking cries of the Indians, the agonized cries of men, the screams of women. What happened next was hazed in her mind. The wagon started to rock and suddenly it toppled over and crashed onto its side. Always Laughing must have banged her head, for she lost consciousness.

The next thing she remembered was when the blanket was snatched away from her and there was an Indian standing over her. At the side was the body of her mother. She was dead. The girl had no time to weep. The Indian picked her up and carried her away.

Later, she learned that her father and all the wagon-folk had been killed except for the six children who were taken captive.

* * *

'You must have been very afraid,' the reverend said.

Always Laughing nodded. 'At first maybe a lot. I cried for my mother and father for a long time. But the Indians were kind to me and eventually I felt as if I was one of them.'

'After a while you were traded to the Osage?'

'Yes,' she said, 'for ten horses. And Big Horse took me into his lodge, treated me like a daughter.'

'And you never married?'

This was one of the rare occasions he saw her frown. 'There was a man I liked, and he liked me. He played an eagle-bone whistle so that Big Horse would know he wished to take me for his woman, and it was agreed he would give twelve horses. It was a good profit because he'd paid only ten horses for me. But the man was killed a week later in a raid on the Comanches, who had now become our enemies.'

She might have wept then, but the reverend rested his hand on hers and said, 'Let us pray for his soul. The Indian heaven is the same place as the white man's heaven.'

She nodded and they knelt, placed their hands together and he spoke the words.

Afterwards she told him how she had grown fond of another man — Joe Vance. The reverend listened closely. Vance had been found by Big Horse and brought back to their village. He had been ill, but she'd nursed him back to health, giving him mescal buttons to chew on. These made him drowsy and eased his pain. When he was fit again she would have gone with him, but Big Horse forbade it because she was still in mourning for the man to whom she had been betrothed.

When she finished the story they were silent for a while, but gradually her sweet, cheerful manner was restored.

As they travelled on he was anxious to make haste, for he was afraid that when they reached the mine, Ironside might already be there and, God forbid, have taken the reward poster literally. Joe Vance wanted . . . *dead* or alive.

He was not to know that events had occurred that were very different from those he imagined.

Always Laughing, whose instincts were honed to Indian sharpness, led the way across the vast desert landscape which was clothed with cacti, agaves, yuccas and later, with big sagebrush. Above, the sky was so blue it almost hurt their eyes to look at it. Small birds were flushed from the mesquite as their horses travelled through it. They paused at water holes and once disturbed a herd of pronghorn deer as they drank.

On the morning of the third day they saw a dust cloud in the distance, which materialized into a hunting party of Comanches. This was not headed towards them, but Always Laughing advised that it would be best to lie low for an hour or so before they went on.

In the afternoon they encountered another water hole. Beyond it was a high, rocky ridge. She pointed excitedly and cried, 'That is the place!'

His breathing quickened, firstly because they had at last arrived, but then because apprehension touched him. Were Joe and Catherine here? Or was Ironside awaiting? The ex-hangman would not take kindly to the fact that Cooper had survived the Comanche torture. He might even shoot him on sight. The reverend was not to know that these immediate fears were unfounded; nor was he to know that other perils awaited him in this place which Always Laughing had called 'evil, full of rattlesnakes'.

The girl indicated that they should leave their horses and proceed on foot. They dismounted, tethered the animals, and she led the way through a scattering of large boulders. Then the gradient became steep beneath their feet. The slope was covered with thick, wiry grass which grew waist high and was so sharp it cut the reverend's hand. As they struggled upward, their faces glistened with sweat. The reverend glanced ahead, seeking the black eye of a cave-entrance in the rock, but he could not see it. He asked the girl to pause, wondering if inside the hidden entrance were other human beings — or just rattlesnakes?

Everything appeared quiet.

They were within yards of the rock face when Always Laughing stumbled but regained her balance. Anxious to discover what awaited them, the reverend scrambled ahead. It was then that the ground seemed to give way beneath his boots and he felt himself falling.

He flailed out with his arms, grasped the sharp blades of grass, but he was fighting a losing battle and was sliding downward. He was aware of an overwhelming, sickly stench. Suddenly his toe found purchase on a slight ledge of rock, arresting his fall. He felt the girl's hands clamp over his arms, gripping his coat. It started to rip, but she altered her hold. Together, they struggled. Gradually he was drawn up. He managed to get his knee over the lip of the hole, and then he was able to haul himself out.

For a moment they lay in the grass, panting with exertion and relief. He felt immensely grateful to the girl. Without her help he felt sure he would have fallen into some murky depths.

'It's like a trap,' he said.

They had risen to their feet, were about to climb on, when they heard a weak cry from below. It was as if a lost spirit was calling out from hell.

* * *

Joe Vance's condition worsened. His wound was infected and his fever had returned. Moreover, he dreamed that the marshal suddenly barged in and

arrested him. In moments of consciousness he knew he had to get out of Pinto
as soon as possible. He grieved over the
fact that Catherine hadn't visited him.
He wondered what power Ironside had
over her. He didn't trust the man but
he was in no condition to do anything
else but play along with him for the
time being. He felt as weak as a kitten,
and any attempt to get out of this
bed would have him collapsing on the
floor.

Doctor Malmuddy changed his dress-
ings twice each day. Augustine bathed
the wound and applied ointments and
this was when the trouble started. Her
groping hands began to wander and she
would draw back the sheet, far more
than necessary, to reveal his nakedness.
Her interest in a man's body went far
beyond the medical aspect.

'Get off,' he would groan, sometimes
when he was conscious and sometimes
when he was in delirium. It was on an
occasion of the latter, as the doctor
rebandaged his shoulder, that Vance

struggled and cried out. Malmuddy waited patiently until his patient was semi-awake, then he posed the question, 'Who?'

Vance's feverish brow puckered, then his lips shaped the name. 'Augustine.'

The doctor swore beneath his breath. Implications began to form in his mind, implications that could make him appear a fool and bring shame on him.

Shortly, he faced his wife in the kitchen. 'Augustine, I have a matter of the utmost importance to discuss with you. I want a straight answer. Have you been pestering Ben?' Ben had been the name Vance had assumed. 'Have you been . . . ?'

'No!' she responded, but her face had reddened and she'd averted her eyes.

'And the other man . . . Duncan?'

'They're m-making up stories,' she stammered.

Malmuddy knew his wife was lying.

'You'll bring shame on me,' he said.

Augustine suddenly lapsed into a torrent of tears. 'I . . . I can't help myself,' she sobbed.

Previously, whenever she'd cried, he had put his arm around her shoulder and comforted her, but now he didn't. He was silent and stern.

He pondered on what he should do. He could either admit that his wife had lied to him, or alternatively he could let Duncan sweat it out in jail and face the charges. He eventually concluded that the latter option would cause him the lesser embarrassment.

Later, in order to draw her husband's thoughts away from her guilt, she told him about the conversation she'd overheard when Ironside had visited.

13

Haycox was in low spirits when he returned to the out-of-town campsite, deeply depressed that Duncan was now in jail. Haycox didn't believe that his friend had raped the girl. As he got a fire going and cooked a lonely meal, his thoughts wandered to the reverend. What had happened to him? Had he been killed by Indians, or maybe succumbed to the desert? Or, best of all, had he found the mine?

After a while he pondered on what he should do in the current situation. Hatred for Ironside burned inside him. He wondered why the ex-hangman was in Pinto and what his intentions were. Haycox wasn't to know that Vance and Catherine were also in the town.

Now, more than ever, he wanted to kill Ironside. He figured he'd wait for evening and then go hunting for him.

* * *

Ironside was equally anxious to trace Haycox. He eventually enquired at the doctor's surgery, and Malmuddy told him he'd heard that Haycox and Duncan had set up camp on the hill overlooking the town. Ironside rode up the hill and soon spotted a spiral of smoke rising from a cooking fire. He dismounted and tethered his horse. He checked his gun and crept forward on foot through the trees. Ten minutes later he was viewing the campsite, hidden by a screen of foliage. Haycox was sprawled on his back beneath the makeshift lean-to, smoking a cigarette.

Ironside yelled out, 'I never killed your brother but I'm gonna kill you!'

Haycox was starting to move as Ironside took aim and fired. The .45 slug struck Haycox in the chest, causing him to yell with agony, pitching him backward and bringing the lean-to collapsing down. Amazingly, he got to his feet, at the same time snatching his gun from its holster and grasping it two-handed. His mouth was wide open, blood running from the side. He took a step forward, thumbing back the hammer, and blasted off a shot. It whined wide.

Unscathed, Ironside fired again. Lead slammed into Haycox's forehead, hurling him back into the wreckage of the lean-to.

Ironside took a deep breath. Then he stepped forward through the haze of gunsmoke. He checked the body and saw the hand move. Two fingers twitched, then stilled. Ironside pointed his gun to fire once more, then realized it would not be necessary. He grunted with satisfaction.

He gathered up the slight burden of Haycox in his strong arms and carried him a quarter-mile until he came to a deep crevice in the rocks. He cast the body into its gloomy depths and felt sure it would not be found in a hurry. He then returned to the campsite, covered up the splashings of blood and dusted over his footprints. He restored the lean-to to its upright position. Any folks who came searching for Haycox would conclude that he had simply left the location.

Ironside returned to the guest house and presently took lunch with the sullen Catherine. Neither of them spoke. She had no doubt that he would keep his word, catch her and beat her if she attempted to wander. After the meal she retired to her room and turned the key. He told himself that he was no longer attracted to her in a physical way, but she was worth money to him.

In the afternoon he went out. He felt an urgency to move things along. The sun was hot and the town was slumbering in its siesta. He purchased a small wagon from the hostelry. He then walked up the deserted Main Street to the doctor's surgery, rang the bell and stepped inside. He was pleased that Malmuddy himself appeared from the side room. Both men nodded a curt greeting.

Ironside said, 'I've got a proposition for you, Doc.'

Malmuddy cocked his head. 'Well?'

'I need to move on. I've lingered here for too long.'

'I hope you settle my bill before you go,' the doctor said. 'Ben will need treatment for maybe two weeks more. That's if his infection clears up.'

'I'll settle the bill all right,' Ironside assured. 'With interest if you accept my proposition.'

The doctor showed a spark of impatience.

'I'm leaving tomorrow,' Ironside said, 'and I intend to take . . . Ben with me!'

Malmuddy threw up his hands in horror. 'You can't do that. If he doesn't get medical treatment he could die.'

'That's what I mean, Doc. We need you to come with us.'

'I can't do that . . . '

'Yes you can. Now listen close. There's a gold mine out in the desert and Ben knows exactly where it is. I need him to show the way. And I need you to make sure he gets the necessary treatment to keep him alive. I'm telling you, there's a fortune in gold waiting out there . . . and half of it can be yours if you come. That's a promise.'

Malmuddy's lips tightened. The fact was that ever since Augustine had told him about what she'd overheard, he had brooded on thoughts of a gold mine in the desert and the things he could do if sudden wealth came his way. But still he protested.

'What about all my patients here? They need a doctor.'

'A few might die,' Ironside said. 'But that don't matter, not when you compare it with what you'd gain.'

Malmuddy's mind was racing. 'You say we'd go fifty-fifty. Is that a promise?'

'Sure it's a promise. You have Ben ready to travel by daylight on Thursday. I've bought a wagon. Make sure you bring all the medical supplies you need.'

The doctor had started to sweat at

the prospect. He swallowed hard and nodded his bald head.

★   ★   ★

It was the afternoon of the next day. Augustine Malmuddy was horrified at the mess she was in. Her husband had spoken about the case going to a court of law; this was something she'd not considered when she'd rashly complained that Duncan had raped her. Her husband had taken it far too seriously. Of course Duncan would deny it. Now the prospect of having to stand up in a courtroom and repeat the lie filled her with the profoundest trepidation. She imagined herself overwhelmed by humiliation, and fainting.

With her husband away visiting a difficult childbirth and an elderly patient, she remained in the bedroom, her mind tortured to the extreme as she tried to think of a way in which she could extricate herself from the torment.

One desperate solution seeped into her thoughts. She whimpered as it gained feasibility.

She rose to her feet and unsteadily made her way through the bedroom doorway, down the stairs and along a corridor to the pharmacy. Its door was locked but on a side hideaway she found the key. Inside were the shelves filled with rows of drugs and medication. She wondered if dying was painful. She looked up to the jars on the top shelf. In bright red lettering they bore the word POISON.

She fetched a small stepladder, climbed it and stretched her hand towards the jar marked ARSENIC. She was trembling so violently that she almost fell. Her extended arm grew leaden.

She cried out in anguish as she realized she couldn't take her own life. Her nerve failed. She stumbled back down the stepladder, collapsing onto the floor, weeping.

Later she returned to the bedroom.

She felt drained of all emotion. Strangely, it was then that an alternative plan probed into her head. She would run away. This time she knew she would go through with it.

She drew together the possessions she would need and packed them in a carpetbag. She knew there was a stagecoach departing at five o'clock that evening for Saint Christopher, where she had an aunt. She would write a note for her husband, pleading with him to forgive her sinful ways, and she would be gone before he returned. But first, there was something else she had to do; she hoped it would defuse the situation and allow some of the shame to be driven from her soul. She would go to the marshal, explain to him that all charges against Duncan should be dropped and there was no point in keeping him in jail any longer.

When she arrived at the lawman's office she found that Marshal Clayburn was away attending a trial up-country. Meanwhile a young deputy, Morris, was in charge. He listened to August-ine's breathless story and blushed. He said he would inform Clayburn when he returned.

'You'll let Duncan free?' she demanded.

He shook his head. 'Don't have the authority for that, ma'am. The marshal will decide when he gets back. That'll be in a few days.'

She gave an exasperated sigh, but then she reckoned the delay wouldn't matter much. At least by the time Duncan was freed, she'd be far away and would never need to see him again.

* * *

Duncan eventually found himself at liberty. He had spent the long boring time behind bars berating the Mal-muddy girl, but on release he decided to do nothing more than avoid her henceforth. His immediate intention was to find Dave Haycox and deter-mine what future action to take. He recovered his horse from the hostelry where Haycox had stabled it, and rode up to the encampment. He was surprised to find it deserted and concluded that perhaps Haycox had gone into town, but on enquiring he drew a blank. Nobody had seen the young man, but he did learn that Ironside and Catherine had booked into the guest house.

Feeling uneasy, he decided to challenge Ironside and find out his intentions.

However, on calling at the guest house he was informed that the big man and the girl had booked out on the morning of the previous day. They'd left with a small wagon. Duncan was surprised that the girl was with Ironside.

Frustrated, Duncan returned to the campsite and spent an hour searching the area for some clue as to Haycox's whereabouts; he unearthed nothing apart from a half-smoked cigarette stub. This was unusual for, being short of money, Haycox treated a smoke as a luxury and always enjoyed it to the final draw. Duncan's uneasiness deepened. He went to Malmuddy's surgery to see if he could find out more, but the place was locked up, a sign on the door reading: DOCTOR CALLED AWAY — PATIENTS SHOULD SEEK MEDICAL CARE IN CRESCENT FALLS. Crescent Falls was the nearest town.

Duncan searched the outskirts of Pinto and soon discovered the wheel-tracks of a light wagon heading towards the desert. Accompanying it were two horseback riders. He decided to gamble that the tracks had been made by Ironside and whoever was with him. Acting on impulse, he was soon heading the same way.

14

The reverend and Always Laughing were shocked by the weird cry that had sounded from the hole. They exchanged puzzled glances, then Cooper edged carefully back towards the spot where he had fallen, parting the grass as he went. Feeling the ground becoming less stable beneath his feet, he stopped. Gingerly, he leaned forward, parting the obscuring grass to reveal the gaping maw-like hole. The sickly stench from it rose about him.

With the herbage drawn back, light shafted twelve feet down into the depths, suddenly revealing what the reverend at first thought to be a skull peering up. Then he realized it was the gauntest of faces. The lips moved. The agonized, parched cry came again.

The reverend called, 'Hold on. We'll get you out!'

He scrambled back to the girl. 'You've got a reata. Go fetch it quick!'

She nodded and hurried down to where the horses were tethered. She grabbed the rawhide rope from her saddle and returned to where the reverend was waiting. He had called to the trapped man several times, but only got a groan in response.

Now he moved quickly. Balancing precariously on the rim, he uncoiled the rawhide and lowered the end into the hole. 'Take hold so we can pull you out,' he cried. No reply came from below, no grabbing of the rope.

Always Laughing had crept up beside the reverend. 'The poor soul's too weak to take hold of the rope,' he said. 'I'll have to go down.'

She gave him a dismayed look. 'Maybe you will get trapped,' she gasped.

He smiled reassuringly. 'The Lord. He'll protect me.'

'The white god must be very strong,' she said.

He nodded towards the root of a mesquite tree. 'Fasten the rope around it,' he said. 'Make it really tight.'

She nodded, but she was uncertain as she did as instructed, fearing that the root might not hold.

He didn't appear to share her misgivings. He was not a young athletic man, but he grasped the rawhide confidently and lowered himself downward, bracing his feet against the wall of the hole. The stench filled his nostrils like a gas. When he dropped to the floor of the place, he found the wizened form of a small man slumped beside him. Close by were the remains of another human, impaled on an up-thrust pole, its top pointed like a spear. The body was decomposed almost to a skeleton and now he saw that it was seething with movement. Maggots!

Cooper realized that he was in a fiendish trap; a hole, some twelve feet deep and eight across, with concave, unscalable sides and a killer-spike jutting from its floor, the hole's opening concealed by the clogging grass. Without help from above, in more ways than one, escape would be impossible.

His attention centred on the poor wretch huddled at his feet. He grasped the man beneath the armpits, finding his bony body almost weightless, but strangely he could feel his heart beating. At that moment the man emitted a groan. Cooper cinched the rawhide around his chest and tied a knot, then he shouted to the girl, 'Pull him up!'

He grunted with satisfaction as the rawhide tautened and slowly the man was hauled upward. He seemed to be recovering his senses because he moved his arms. A minute later he reached the top and Always Laughing pulled him to safety.

Cooper glanced around, feeling like a beetle trapped in a jar. He was nigh suffocated by the terrible smell. He wondered how long the other man had been incarcerated, without water or food. The ghastly possibility that he had survived by cannibalizing the other poor victim entered his mind. Now he became aware of his own vulnerability. He had expected Always Laughing to lower the rope immediately and drag him out, but she had not. He trusted her implicitly and yet . . .

His voice was desperate as he yelled her name, repeating it twice, louder each time.

There was no reply.

★ ★ ★

He was a small wraith of a man, his clothing ragged and filthy. Always Laughing had dragged him clear of the hole, and his arms were flailing with surprising strength for one thought to be so close to death. As he glimpsed the feathers in her hair and the buckskin garb, his demented eyes widened with terror, and he spat out one word like a serpent's hiss: 'Injun!'

His arm struck her a bruising blow across the face and she was thrown back. At first her rolling fall was cushioned by grass, but then her head connected with a hidden rock and she remembered nothing else.

★ ★ ★

Ironside rode forward to a slight elevation which gave him a view of the surrounding sun-baked landscape. He saw no movement apart from the heat shimmer. He glanced back and watched the small canvas-topped wagon lumbering along. Vance was sitting propped up beside Catherine on the seat, and the doctor was acting as an outrider.

Their slow pace annoyed Ironside, but Malmuddy had insisted that if they pushed any harder it would be to the detriment of his patient — and they definitely needed Vance to point the way in this godforsaken land.

Yesterday, they had been puzzled by a loud buzzing noise like the humming of a sawmill. As Ironside had ridden forward through dense mesquite, the sound rose to a din. He reached a clearing and saw an Indian burial scaffold, supported by four poles. It had not been weathered by time; it must have been erected recently.

Flies were responsible for the noise: a multitude of giant bluebottles, swarming in a cloud about the horse's head, which was tied to one of the poles. It was decorated with feathers; everything was blackened by swarming insects. The decapitation had been clumsily done. The animal's long tail adorned another pole.

Fanning away flies, Ironside craned his neck for a better view. Upon the scaffold's platform of crossed boughs, some eight feet from the ground, was a blanket-shrouded bundle — obviously a corpse. It had been left to dry out before burial.

The scaffold was a grim reminder that Indians were around. He grunted uneasily. He was still wary of Comanches who might be hungering for his scalp, particularly if they'd discovered that he had gunned down four of their comrades. If attack came, he knew that his own companions would be of little help because they were unarmed. He had made sure of that, for he feared that if they had guns, they might turn them on him.

Now, he was irritated by the doctor's fussiness, but the medical man was useful in keeping Vance alive. He had said that one of Vance's lungs had collapsed. Although the outlaw had taken to riding on the wagon's seat and indicating the way, he was still weak and had developed a cough. Meanwhile Catherine was showing a marked indifference towards him, lapsing into a sullen silence.

When Ironside rejoined the others his gaze dwelt upon the doctor. Once they reached the gold mine, he would have no further use for him. He certainly had no intention of sharing the treasure with him. He reckoned he could kill him, and Vance too, for that matter. But then he had second thoughts. He would have to return to Pinto to register his claim, and questions about the doctor's absence might be asked. The medical man had been seen leaving Pinto in the company of Ironside, and that astute fellow of a marshal might put two and two together. Allowing Malmuddy to live would also pose a problem; Ironside would have to resolve it, one way or another.

As for Vance, Ironside would be taking him back to town, preferably dead, to claim the reward. And once he had returned Catherine to her father, then spent a few months extracting gold from the rock, his wealth would be assured.

That night, as they camped beneath the stars, Ironside stepped out into the mesquite, mounting guard on a slight hillock.

Vance had his bed fixed up in the wagon, while Catherine slept beneath it, between the wheels. As ever, she detested sleeping on the ground but there was no option, for she would not lie alongside Vance. The doctor bedded down on the other side of the small fire.

She lay awake, listening to coyotes serenading the night and praying that no creepy-crawlies would disturb her. She thought of the pampering comforts she'd had in Baltimore and at home. She'd never dreamed that she'd be reduced to the purgatory she currently endured. She missed her mother and sister. If only she'd not despised her father so much! She'd grabbed blindly at Joe Vance's promises of escape. Now, to the very depths of her soul, she hated Jason Ironside.

However the prospect of gleaning some share of the gold could make everything worthwhile.

She was dozing when something nudged her arm; she cried out in fright, but a hand across her mouth stifled further sound. Suddenly Vance's wheezy voice sounded. 'Catherine, be quiet. Listen to me. Get Ironside's gun when he goes to sleep. Bring it to me.'

'Why . . . why do you want it?' she asked.

'I'm gonna kill the son of a bitch.'

She recoiled. 'There's no need to use coarse language,' she said.

He made no response but drew away. He paused to rest; the effort he'd made in coming to her in his weakened state had exhausted him. Then the wagon creaked as he climbed back into it. She heard him cough several times, after which there was silence.

She forced her eyes to remain open, her mind churning over what he had said. She propped herself up, gazing out through the spokes of a wheel. It was two hours later when Ironside returned, like a shadow, to the campsite. She saw him rouse Malmuddy whose turn it now was for sentry-go. The doctor rose from his blankets and shortly disappeared into the darkness.

Ironside went to his own bedroll and turned in. She waited, a tremble growing within her. Presently the steady rhythm of his snoring sounded. She resorted to counting his consecutive snores. When she reached a hundred she steeled herself to make a move. She knew that he always slept with his gunbelt on the ground, close to his head within easy reach.

How delighted she would be if he were dead. If only she could stop her trembling.

She was thankful that the moon was obscured by cloud and the glimmer of the fire had died. She could hear the stirrings of the horses, hobbled some yards away. Crouching low, she crept towards Ironside's blanketed form, glimpsing the darker shape of the gunbelt where she'd expected it to be. As she groped for it, his snoring stopped. Her heart missed a beat. She stepped back. To her horror, he sat up and he was staring directly at her.

15

Jake Simpson's deranged senses had accepted his miraculous escape from the hole in the belief that an angel had descended from Heaven and brought about his salvation. But his euphoria was soon dispelled by the sight of Indian feathers, the tanned skin, and the horrific recollections that stabbed into his mind. Lashing out with his arm had been instinctive. He felt no gratitude for the person who had pulled him from the depths, but only the terror that he might soon lose his scalp. He was not even aware that she was a girl. And he felt crazy with the anxiety that other Indians could be close by. His main wish was to get away from this ghastly place with all possible haste and never return.

His weakened legs practically gave out as he stumbled down the hill, tearing his way through the thick grass. Suddenly he came upon the water hole and splashed into it. He glanced back furtively, then cupped water to his lips and drank long and hard. Finishing, he became aware of the two horses tethered nearby by the reverend and Always Laughing. He ran to them and ripped the reins of the foremost animal from the foliage, half falling as he did so. Panic gave him strength. He dragged himself up on to the Indian saddle, ramming hard with his heels. The beast took off like a charge of canister. Simpson had only a vague idea of where they were headed. All that mattered was that he was getting away.

It had been some years ago when his mining partner Chad Brimmer had told him about the gold mine. However, before they salvaged gold, Brimmer had claimed he had an important appointment to keep in Barn Springs. It was with the woman he intended to marry. He departed, telling Simpson to wait for his return when they would go into partnership and exploit their good luck. He'd left Simpson with vague instructions for finding the mine. But Brimmer had been jilted. His woman had run off with her new lover. He'd tracked them down and murdered them both. But the law caught up with him and he had suffered justice at the end of a rope, courtesy of Jason Ironside.

Jake Simpson had been smitten with a consumptive chest and had been laid low for what seemed an eternity. He came close to death himself, but he never forgot about the mine. When at last he was back on his feet, he'd set out to find it. However Brimmer's map was inexact. Simpson had wandered the desert, been tortured by Indians and escaped. But eventually he located what he sought.

Then he stumbled on something about which Brimmer hadn't enlightened him: the trap he'd fashioned to protect the place from intruders. Simpson dropped like a falling rock, only saved from impaling himself on the up-thrust spike by the fact that he had fallen close to the wall. He was not the first victim of the hole. Some other poor soul had plunged to his death.

It wasn't long before he discovered that the concave nature of the walls prevented him from clambering out. He expected he would die of thirst.

Now his place in the hole had been taken by another man. The reverend had clawed frantically at the concave walls, seeking a handhold, but there was nothing and eventually he dropped to the floor, wearied by his futile effort. He wondered again for how long the other poor wretches had existed in this trap — for that was what it surely was. He also wondered about his own life expectancy. And what had happened to Always Laughing? He tried to fashion an optimistic answer but he failed.

All at once he reproached himself. What would be would be, and he had no right to question. In the past he had sinned, as any man will, and perhaps this was what he was being punished for. Nonetheless, he knelt and prayed, asking the Lord's forgiveness.

Should he die here, his great regret was that he would be unable to complete his mission of preventing Ironside from committing murder. He had no fear of death himself, but he would not have chosen such a dismal end to his life. He might last for days in this hole before he passed on. But if it was God's will, then who was he to question it?

After he had finished praying he felt something crawling over his hand and, glancing down, he saw in the gloom the grotesque form of a scorpion, its sting looped over its back. He flicked it away. He was fortunate that there were no snakes here.

He slumped down against the wall. He looked at the opening above. It looked so near, yet he knew he had no way of reaching it. Only a narrow glimmer of light was admitted, and this was made pale by the grass that had grown over the hole. He would try to sleep.

When he awoke, feeling stiff and with a sense of nausea, he was in complete darkness and he knew that night had come. Already thirst was gnawing at his throat. He was debating whether to pray again, when the girl's voice came. 'Enoch, are you there?'

He rose immediately, hope surging through him. 'Yes! Yes!'

'I'll lower the rope,' she called.

Within ten minutes of hard sweat, he was out of the trap, embracing Always Laughing with all the joy in his heart.

'The man hit me,' she explained. 'I fell, hit my head on a rock. My head aches real bad.'

'But we're still alive,' he cried out. 'Let's thank the Lord!'

Presently, they went down the hill and discovered that one of their horses, together with the parfleche of food it carried, was missing; so was the man they had rescued.

But the reverend was beyond worrying. He was so glad to have escaped from the hole.

'Let's rest now,' he said. 'In the morning, we'll explore the mine. That's if your headache is better.'

★ ★ ★

All those hard-won miles away, at the Hennessey home, Catherine's father Edward had lost plenty of sleep over the shame his daughter had brought on the family. Talk of it had gone through Barn Springs like flame through dry tinder. Now, he seldom ventured into town apart from meetings to do with the election of the next state governor, and already he saw his chances of success slipping away. He would spend hours sitting in a rocking-chair on the veranda of his house, chomping on his cigar and gazing out into the desert. He figured he should have had some news back from the posse by this time. The silence and stress of the situation depressed him.

One morning he rose late and stood for a long time on the veranda. Emily, his wife, was in the kitchen when she heard a thump. Rushing out in alarm, she found her husband collapsed. He was shaking violently and hyperventilating. After a minute she helped him up and guided him into the bedroom to lie down. His skin was grey. He had had these attacks before and she recognized the symptoms. She sent her younger daughter, Rebecca, to town to call Doctor Carter. It was an hour before he arrived. By this time Edward had calmed somewhat. The doctor examined him and confirmed that he'd had a heart attack. He supplied medication and prescribed bed-rest for four days, after which he would return. He then departed.

By this time Edward had perked up, his stubborn nature returning. He reached out, grasped Emily's hand. 'It'll take more than a heart attack to finish me,' he growled. 'Only a bolt of lightning will do that, and it would take two strikes at least!'

★ ★ ★

Through the heat, Duncan followed the tracks of the wagon. He was greatly concerned about the fate of Dave Haycox. He suspected that Ironside was somehow involved. And he was determined to catch up with him and find out the truth. It was clear that the wagon was moving slowly, and he found evidence of two overnight campsites.

Other concerns plagued him. What had happened to the reverend . . . and Vance and the girl? Were they all dead? He pressed on, urging his mount for greater speed.

16

Catherine was horrified when Ironside sat up in his blankets and glared at her. She felt as if all her blood had drained away.

'What are you doing?' he demanded and in the darkness she could see the glint of his teeth and guessed he was snarling.

'What are you doing?' he repeated in a louder voice, his anger growing.

'Oh, J-Jason,' she stammered. 'I felt cold and lonely. I just wanted to curl up in your arms and to feel your warmth.'

He grunted with disbelief.

'It's the truth,' she said.

There was a pause, then his manner seemed to soften. 'Well . . . you better come here.'

He held up the blanket for her to join him.

'Oh, Jason,' she murmured, and

picking up her courage, she slid down beside his hard body and he pulled the blanket over them.

She found what followed horrendous, for his big hands ripped away her clothing and pawed her body. He eased his considerable weight on top of her, pressing his lips against hers. He was like a hungry animal as their teeth connected. She felt suffocated. The smell of him was awful. She would have cried out but she knew it would be to no avail. He took her, over and over, until he was satiated, then he rolled from her and lay back, his breath coming in gusts.

After a long while, he said, 'Go back to your bed. Thank your lucky stars I believed you.'

Feeling utterly bruised, she left him, while he made sure his gun was tucked safely beneath him.

* * *

Next morning they started out early, the sun rising from their left. Ironside had taken the lead, Malmuddy riding on the flank. Catherine drove the wagon. Joe Vance had not risen from his bed, but he was coughing constantly, getting on her nerves. Still, nothing was as bad as what she'd experienced the previous night.

It was mid-morning, and they had just quit a water hole, when Ironside saw the dust rising into the sky. Soon he heard a sound like muted thunder, but it rapidly grew until it filled his ears. He knew from experience what it was and he didn't like it. His horse was tossing its head with panic.

He spurred back towards the wagon. 'Take cover!' he yelled. 'Buffalo on the stampede. They're headed this way!'

Malmuddy nodded his understanding and waved for the wagon to pull over to a slight depression at the side. It was desperately inadequate but there was no other choice. White-faced, Catherine hauled on the reins and managed to guide the wagon as instructed.

The air was becoming tainted with a

musky smell. Ahead of them the dust seemed to explode like a dense fog, out of which came a surging blackness, flowing like lava from a volcano. This was soon revealed as a mass of huge woolly heads and horns.

They were cumbersome animals with massive forequarters and humped shoulders. They were approaching so swiftly, making for the water, that Ironside had no time to rejoin the others. He dropped from the saddle and dragged his horse into the scant cover provided by a mesquite clump. The pounding of hoofs was deafening, the muskiness almost tangible. The buffalo were suddenly all around, brushing against the mesquite, their breath scorching.

Ironside hugged the ground, his head pressed against his forearms. He cursed. It seemed crazy, having come through what he had, to be trampled to death by a herd of thirsty brutes. He had no idea what had happened to the others.

Suddenly a great beast surged through his cover and leaped over him, its trailing hoof kicking him across the shoulder. He cringed into a ball, expecting more to follow, trampling him to a pulp. He felt he was on a small islet, surrounded by a tempestuous sea that was likely to overwhelm him at any moment. Another beast leaped over him. He remained where he was, fearing that more beasts might come crashing through the mesquite. But none came. There was a slackening in the intensity of pounding hoofs and he realized that the herd was drawing off to his left.

Meanwhile Catherine had remained on the seat of the halted wagon as beasts rushed along the edges of the depression, some of them coming down to brush against the wagon and set it rocking. The racket hurt her ears. She was petrified. She clutched her handkerchief to her face, scarcely able to breathe. Vance appeared from behind her, peering out. And then the worst happened.

The two horses harnessed to the

wagon suddenly panicked and took off in a mad gallop. Vance was thrown back. Catherine screamed as the reins were jerked from her grasp. She was tossed about like a rag doll. The wagon bounced madly over the rugged ground, even the buffaloes moving from its path. Suddenly the girl lost her hold on the handrail and was thrown off. She hit the ground and lay still. The wagon careered on until it plunged into a depression, and toppled onto its side, smashing a wheel, ripping away the canvas. The dust rose about it as it came to a shuddering halt, the horses struggling in a tangle of harness.

Some of the buffaloes had reached the water hole, were surging around it, jostling for space. Bulls, cows and calves were nose-dipping and pushing each other. Others, in their masses, crowded behind them, impatiently waiting to drink. Ironside was worried that the herd might return the way it had come, but at least the immediate danger had passed. With the dust beginning to settle, he gazed towards the depression and realized that the wagon was no longer there.

It took two hours for the herd to slake its thirst. Afterwards, the animals moved on, thankfully not turning back.

When all appeared safe, Ironside rose from his cover. He spotted Malmuddy. He must have managed to escape being trampled in a similar way to him. The doctor saw him and waved frantically. Ironside ran over the hoof-torn ground to join him.

About a hundred yards off they saw the canopy of the wagon, flapping unattached in the breeze. As they rushed towards it they found Catherine rising unsteadily to her feet. She pointed ahead of her. They ran on and saw the wagon lying on its side in the depression.

Ironside reached the wrecked vehicle first. The two horses, still in their traces, were trembling. One appeared to have broken its leg.

Malmuddy, panting hard from the

effort of running, saw Ironside descend into the depression, then reappear a moment later, his voice carrying clearly.

'I think Vance is dead!'

Hobbling painfully, Catherine joined the doctor and they went forward to where Ironside was crouching over the prostrate body of the outlaw. Like the girl, Vance had been thrown clear of the wagon. The doctor knelt down beside him, felt his pulse and listened to his chest. When he straightened up, he said, 'He's still alive, but I don't know for how long.'

Ironside growled with anguish. 'You mustn't let him die. We need him.'

Malmuddy glanced at him scornfully.

*   *   *

Next morning, the reverend and Always Laughing climbed to the rock-face and discovered a crevice. The girl said this was the entrance to the mine. It was scarcely wide enough to enter. They carried mesquite that they had twisted to form brands. Now, he watched her patiently, admiring the way she made fire by rubbing sticks together. Within minutes their torches were alight and she squeezed through the tight opening and disappeared inside. He followed quickly, almost getting stuck but eventually making it. They found themselves in a small cave. In its depths another cave led off. A cold, dank smell permeated the air.

The reverend raised his torch and examined the surrounding walls. He saw the yellow veins spreading over them.

'Untapped gold!' he cried out, unable to suppress the riffle of excitement that spread through him. 'Gold has always been treasured by man.'

Always Laughing nodded but he could tell she was nervous. 'Watch for snakes,' she warned.

He paced forward and entered the far opening, the flame from his torch setting shadows dancing on roof and walls. Natural tunnels led out from the second chamber like an ants' nest. His foot touched something and he stooped to pick it up. 'A solid piece of gold,' he said. He slipped it into his pocket.

He moved on into one of the tunnels. The roof grew lower, and he cracked his head against a downward-jutting rock. He dropped to his knees, stunned as dizziness swept through him. He would have cursed had he been a cursing man, but he was not.

Always Laughing came up behind him and helped him to his feet; it was then that they heard the warning buzz of a rattlesnake. It filled the cave with angry, vibrating sound. The intrusion into its hiding-place had incensed the creature. In the flickering light the reverend glimpsed the spade-shaped head rearing up. The tongue was spitting probingly into space.

The dizziness drained from Cooper like whiskey from a broken bottle. He ushered the girl ahead of him and together they scampered back the way they had come. They were glad when they had squeezed through the hole and out into the sun's heat.

★ ★ ★

Catherine felt annoyed. She'd fallen from the wagon and could have broken every bone in her body, yet Malmuddy was giving all his attention to Joe Vance. Presently, Ironside recovered the canvas top and he and the doctor rigged up a cover to protect the outlaw from the sun. Only then did Malmuddy turn to examine the girl. He had her moving her limbs and confirmed that she had no bones broken, although her left hip was badly bruised, which would make walking difficult.

Meanwhile Ironside checked the wagon, seeing that it was damaged beyond recall, with a wheel and the wagon-bed smashed. The two horses that had been in harness had now calmed, though one had clearly broken its leg and would be useless. In the meanest of moods, Ironside stepped across to the injured horse, drew his pistol and pressed the muzzle into its ear. When he pulled the trigger the horse dropped, causing him to leap back. Catherine screamed, having no taste for the slaughter of creatures.

The animals that Ironside and Malmuddy had been riding had disappeared, the girl couldn't walk and Vance, being at death's door, was in no condition to guide them. Furthermore, there could be Indians on the prowl. Ironside himself was completely lost and he was foul-mouthed with anger. There seemed no hope in their predicament.

17

Catherine's body hurt all over, especially her hip. She had been given some opiates by the doctor, but these hadn't helped much. He had now returned to the canvas shelter and was fussing over Joe Vance, who appeared to be still unconscious. Ironside sat a little way off, his head slumped as he blasphemed, muttered his frustrations and sometimes dozed.

Catherine glanced up, seeing how the landscape shimmered in the heat. Her gaze focused on a dot in the far distance; it was bobbing up and down. At first she figured that her eyes were playing tricks, or maybe it was some sort of mirage. She felt puzzled, then she grew afraid as realization came to her.

'There's a rider coming,' she cried. 'Could be an Indian!'

Ironside snapped to wakefulness. He came to his feet and gazed in the direction she pointed.

'Who the hell . . . ?' he exclaimed.

Malmuddy joined them and they all strained their eyes to discover who was approaching. Sure enough they shortly discerned a rider slowly getting closer. To their relief he certainly wasn't an Indian. He was a small white man who was skeletal in appearance and was without a hat, which was crazy with the sun so torrid. At last he reached them, reined in, promptly slipped from the back of his pony and sank to the ground. After a moment he sat up, his sunken eyes taking them in.

'Who are you?' Ironside demanded.

The reply came in a weak voice. 'I'm Jake Simpson. Pleased to make your acquaintance. Could I please have some water?'

Doctor Malmuddy fetched him a canteen and he drank noisily. When he'd finished he wiped his lips with the back of his scrawny hand.

'What are you doing in this god-damned desert?' Ironside asked, his glare showing no mercy.

Simpson said, 'I'm just a simple miner who fell down a hole and nearly died of thirst.'

'A hole?' Malmuddy queried.

Simpson nodded. 'Sure. Some son-of-a-bitch dug a hole big enough to trap a man. I just couldn't get out, not until an angel came down from heaven and rescued me.'

Ironside snorted with disbelief. A thought came to him. 'This hole . . . where was it?'

'Way off to the south,' Simpson explained, 'right close to the Rattle-snake Mine. I never want to go near that hell of a place again.'

Ironside's mind was racing. 'What were you looking for?'

'Why, gold of course. That's what I was looking for.'

'Then you know where this Rattle-snake Mine is?' Ironside said. 'You could take us there?'

'Of course I know where the goddamned mine is, but I'm not going back there, not in a thousand years, not for you or nobody else. I'm headed for Pinto.'

To Catherine's surprise Ironside drew his gun. He thumbed back the hammer and pointed it at their visitor. 'I think you'll take us there, that's unless you want to die here and now!'

An expression of astonishment spread across Simpson's bony features. He looked like a dwarf with Ironside looming over him. He gazed into the borehole of the pistol, his eyes wide with fear. He seemed momentarily speechless.

'You *will* take us there,' Ironside repeated, his voice as harsh as rock, and it was a statement that brooked no argument.

★ ★ ★

The reverend and the girl worked hard. Both were sporting large bruises: Cooper had a bump on his head which felt like

191

an egg, while Always Laughing's face was badly swollen and she had lost a tooth. But now they forgot their discomfort and toiled up and down the hill, carrying boulders as large as they could manage. These they dumped into the hole, taking infinite care not to fall in themselves. Gradually the trap was filled, entombing the corpse of the poor individual who had been impaled. The reverend had no idea of his identity but he said a prayer for his soul. He assumed he was some prospector who had stumbled onto the mine and paid the awful penalty. At least now the trap would claim no more victims.

Cooper was bitterly disappointed. He had hoped to find Vance, Catherine and Ironside here but there was no sign of them. There was a possibility that they had come to this place and killings had occurred; this worried him, but he had found no evidence of any encampment.

He and the girl had only one horse left and future travel would be difficult. He decided that the best thing would be to remain where they were in the hope that the others might turn up. In the meantime he would use the power of prayer to seek guidance.

★　★　★

Duncan had stuck doggedly to the wagon's tracks until eventually they became completely obliterated by the hoofprints of buffaloes. Feeling frustrated, he spent the night resting near a water hole, but he pressed on at the first hint of daylight. He headed south, guided by raw instinct. He wished he had the reverend's faith to show him the way, although he was unsure what had happened to the minister.

Nonetheless, by incredible chance, he came upon the distant sight of the wrecked wagon and the figures grouped around it. Not knowing whom he would find, he urged his horse forward and presently reached what was a temporary campsite. There was mutual astonishment all round as recognition dawned. There was no warmth in their curt greetings.

Duncan suspected that Ironside was responsible for Dave Haycox's disappearance, but he decided not to broach the subject for the moment. He was surprised to see Catherine. There was another man, a stranger, the scrawniest individual Duncan had ever seen. He looked furtive, sometimes glancing in Ironside's direction as though he was frightened of him.

Then Doctor Malmuddy stepped from the canvas shelter. He was shaking his head and looking downright solemn. 'Joe Vance has just died,' he said.

Ironside cursed. Catherine showed no emotion. She looked completely drained.

'What are we going to do?' she asked.

'We're gonna push on to the mine,' Ironside said. 'Our friend Simpson'll show us the way. We've got two horses now and we'll cut up the dead one for meat.'

Catherine shuddered but she said nothing more.

Within an hour they were on the move, having buried Vance in a shallow grave. Simpson was on foot in the lead. He stumbled frequently, but attracted no sympathy. Ironside came next, astride the Indian pony that Simpson had arrived on. Catherine was riding Duncan's horse while he walked alongside her. Following at the back was Malmuddy, clutching his bag of medications and wishing for all the world that he had stayed in Pinto — gold or no gold.

★　★　★

Miles away another world seemed to exist. The Hennessey house was silent apart from the ticking and hourly chimes of the fine grandfather clock. There was about the place an air of waiting; but still no news had come from the posse or Catherine. Mrs Emily Hennessey fetched Doctor Carter a drink of buttermilk whilst he saw to her husband upstairs. Edward had suffered a further and more serious heart attack.

When the doctor came downstairs she knew that the news wasn't good by his grave manner. They sat at the table sipping their drinks.

'Emily,' the doctor said in a hushed voice, 'medication can only do so much good. I'm afraid he can't last much longer. You should prepare yourself for the worst. I would reserve a plot at the cemetery in town.'

She nodded her acceptance of the cold facts.

★   ★   ★

Far away across the desert, on the hill overlooking Pinto, Marshal Clayburn had been puzzled by the circling of buzzards. When he rode up he found that the birds had been drawn to a deep crevice in the rocks. They had landed but they rose up indignantly as he approached. He peered down into the fissure. A smell of decomposition was hanging in the air. He could just distinguish what remained of a body in the depths. With his suspicions mounting, he went back into town and called out four of his deputies. Within two hours they had hauled up the corpse. Clayburn recognized, by the clothing, that this was the young man he'd detained overnight in his jail, having arrested him in the saloon.

The body was wrapped in a blanket, conveyed back to town and deposited in the mortuary. Knowing of the bitter feud that had existed between Haycox and Ironside, Clayburn took out an arrest warrant for Ironside.

18

'Enoch,' Always Laughing cried out, 'there's somebody coming!'

The reverend sat by a small fire finishing his supper, consisting of the roebuck that the girl had killed with an arrow. Now, in haste, he licked his fingers and stood up.

The two of them hurried to where they had a better vantage point and saw the straggling procession approaching below them, a procession that materialized into the familiar figures of Jason Ironside, Duncan and Catherine. Bringing up the rear were Doctor Malmuddy and the diminutive Jake Simpson. They shared only two horses, and those walking looked utterly exhausted.

Cooper and Always Laughing scrambled down the hill to meet them.

Duncan and the reverend embraced each other with genuine delight. The other newcomers, after surprise at the reunion had evaporated, sank to the ground. The latter miles of their journey, mostly on foot, had brought them to the end of their tether.

Duncan watched Ironside, seeing that the big man showed no pleasure at finding the reverend here. In fact he looked downright mean.

As explanations unfolded, Ironside remained silent. Always Laughing lit a fire and cooked more of the roebuck, after which the newcomers scorched their lips as they assuaged their hunger. Meanwhile night was sifting down about them.

But now the reverend asked a question. 'Where's Joe Vance?'

Malmuddy exchanged a glance with Ironside, then said, 'He died. He'd been shot pretty badly, and he fell from the wagon we had. It was all too much for him and he passed away.'

The effect on the reverend was profound. He emitted a sob, his shoulders sagged and he dropped his head. After a moment he straightened up and in a strained voice he asked another question. 'Shot by whom?'

On defiant impulse Catherine suddenly spoke up. 'Ironside shot him.'

All eyes swung to the ex-hangman. 'Sure I shot him,' he proclaimed arrogantly. 'He was wanted dead or alive. I did the community a service.'

Duncan then saw something he'd never dreamed he'd see. Just for a moment a gaze of unmitigated maliciousness blazed from the reverend's eyes, and it was directed at Ironside. But quickly Cooper turned away, rose to his feet and walked off.

Duncan rose and followed him. He found him kneeling beyond a clump of mesquite, kneeling with his head bowed, his hands steepled in prayer. Out of respect, Duncan waited in silence. He knew that the reverend had come on this mission in order to save life, but he'd failed and he was taking it mighty hard.

After a long while the prayer was

finished; Duncan went forward and dropped to his knees alongside the other man. 'I'm sorry,' he said.

Cooper cleared his throat and said, 'I guess it's God's will, and I've got to accept it. I came on this terrible journey to save Joe's life.'

Duncan said nothing, feeling that any comment from him would be an intrusion.

'You see,' the reverend said, 'I was his . . . father.'

Duncan gasped with surprise. 'His father?'

The reverend nodded. 'It was a long time ago, when I had a dear wife and a family.' His voice gave out, choked by sadness.

They waited. From behind them they could hear the muted voices of the others.

'Tell me,' Duncan murmured.

'We lived in New York, but we were desperately poor, so we decided to chance our luck in the West. There were so many glowing reports. I went on first and eventually got a good job as a teacher. I sent for my family, but when they were travelling up the Lake Eerie Canal they were ambushed by river pirates. They were all drowned . . . apart from Joe, who was just three years old. At first I thought that he'd been drowned alongside his ma and sisters. But he was taken by the pirates and brought up to a life of crime. I only found out the truth years later.'

'And what did you do?' Duncan prompted.

'Losing my family hit me hard. I lost my way, took to gambling, drink and women. But one night the Lord came to me in a dream. He gave me solace and showed me the path I should take. So I entered the church and realized the Lord's wisdom. A couple of years back, Joe somehow found out where I was living. Taking a great risk, because he was a wanted outlaw, he visited me, and he said that one day he would give himself up and accept his punishment. Now he can never do that.'

Duncan said, 'Ironside . . . what will you do about him? Can you ever forgive him?'

The reverend fell silent again. Duncan saw that he was clenching and unclenching his fingers, the nails pressing into his palms. When he spoke his voice came with a new conviction. 'The Lord will guide me. I will accept his will.'

After they rejoined the main party everybody bedded down for the night. Ironside had decided that he would enter the mine in the morning. He made it clear he wanted no company.

★   ★   ★

Everybody was astir soon after dawn. Always Laughing rekindled the fire and set about slicing off some meat for breakfast.

Jake Simpson sidled across towards the reverend. 'I said sorry to the Injun girl,' he said. 'I shouldn't have hit her like I did, but I'm dead scared of Injuns, and I guess my brain was addled. She told me it was you who pulled me out of that hole. If it hadn't been for you, I'd be dead by now. So I'm saying a big thank you.'

The reverend nodded and said, 'It was the Lord's will.'

'Well, I'm right grateful to whoever was responsible,' Simpson said, then he added, 'There was one other thing. I never went into the mine myself. Fell down that goddamned hole before I could. But the Indian girl told me you salvaged a nugget o' gold from it.'

'Why, sure,' Cooper said. He had it in his pocket and had forgotten all about it. He fetched it out and handed it to Simpson, who examined it carefully, turning it over. He sniffed it. He next asked the reverend if he had a knife, but he hadn't. However, the reverend went across to Always Laughing and borrowed hers. He handed it to Simpson.

As he did so, he noticed that Ironside was watching them.

To his surprise, Simpson rubbed the

blade of the knife quite fiercely against the nugget, producing some sparks.

'I'll be damned,' Simpson said. 'Well that's sure proof. It reeks of sulphur and it's the best example of fool's gold I ever did see. Iron pyrite . . . absolutely worthless!'

Overhearing them, Ironside seemed to explode. 'No! No!' he cried. 'It's a lie!' He stepped forward, his face working with fury. He struck Simpson a blow across the face, knocking the little man off his feet. 'You're trying to trick me,' he snarled. 'That mine belongs to me. I'll prove the gold is real!'

He stormed off to where the fire was, snatched up one of the torches that Always Laughing had prepared, then he climbed the hill, forcing his way through the high grass. He soon disappeared.

Meanwhile Doctor Malmuddy busied himself, passing out ointment for the bruised Simpson and the sore feet of Catherine. Duncan marvelled at the doctor's bag. It seemed to contain medication for every ailment.

Presently the reverend conducted a short service. With heads bowed, the small gathering prayed that they would have a safe journey home. They also prayed for the souls of the departed.

An hour had passed before Malmuddy remarked that Ironside had not returned from his visit to the mine. Duncan decided to go and look for him and the reverend said he would come as well. Taking brands and matches given them by the doctor, they ascended the hill and reached the crevice in the rock face. Here, they lit their torches.

Duncan squeezed into the interior first, breathing in the cold, dank air. *Beware of snakes,* he thought. Behind him, Cooper struggled through the narrow opening. Step by step Duncan went forward. He had the feeling that he was being sucked into the gloom. He called out Ironside's name, but the only response was the eerie echo. He flinched as he glimpsed movement to his left, but he relaxed; he realized it was merely shadow.

Then he heard the buzzing sound. It throbbed through the gloom and he knew it was not the rattle of a snake. It was if a million wings were beating.

'What's that?' he gasped.

'Heaven knows,' the reverend responded.

The sound seemed to be coming from the inner cave.

At that moment a scream sounded — an eruption of stark terror, repeated over and over until it was drowned out by the unearthly buzz.

19

For a moment Duncan's instinct was to get out of this place as fast as he could, but then he realized that somebody, presumably Ironside, was in trouble, big trouble. Swallowing hard, he paced into the narrow tunnel that led to the inner cave. As the torch spread its flickering light, his eyes seized upon the huddled figure on the floor. It seemed to be covered by a seething black mass. And now the air about Duncan came alive with fluttering, insistent movement. Huge insects!

Waving the torch before him, he ran to the body, stooped down and rolled it over. It was Ironside all right, but he was scarcely recognizable. His face and head were completely covered by the swarming creatures.

Cooper appeared alongside. 'Let's get him out of here,' he cried.

They grabbed Ironside beneath the armpits and dragged his heavy body back into the tunnel, the insects flying into them angrily. In that panicking moment Duncan dropped his torch. There was no time to gather it up.

Suddenly he felt a stabbing pain in his hand. It was like an electric shock which grew in intensity until it became a fierce agony that had him yelling out and letting go of Ironside. Manfully, Cooper carried on dragging the dead weight until Duncan once again assisted him, but the agony was seeping up his arm, paralysing it.

They reached the opening, tried to force Ironside through. He was too bulky. How he'd entered in the first place was a mystery. Insects still blundered into them.

'We'll have to leave him,' Duncan gasped. 'Let's get out.'

They dropped their burden. There was no time for courtesies. The reverend went first, grazing himself on the rock. Duncan followed and they scrambled in unashamed haste down the hill.

At the bottom, they realized that some of the insects were clinging to their clothing. Their blue bodies were two inches long, their wings rust-coloured, their long legs had hooked claws and an evil stinger protruded from the tail.

As Duncan and the reverend were carefully brushing them off, Malmuddy came rushing up. He gazed at them aghast. Then he peered closely at one of the creatures.

'Tarantula hawk wasps,' he announced, 'better known as giant cazadores. They attack in swarms. Their sting is worse than any other insect.'

'I know,' Duncan said.

'The pain lasts for about five minutes, giving a feeling of paralysis, then it gets easier.'

It was two hours before they returned to the crevice. This time they brought Always Laughing's rawhide rope. When Duncan re-entered the interior most of the insects seemed to have departed. He got the rope around Ironside and with much effort they pulled him through the hole.

When he was laid out on the ground, he was a ghastly sight. His face, throat, lips, eyelids and head were puffed up like an angry-red balloon. The swarm must have completely covered him at one stage. No doubt they'd stung through his clothing as well.

'I guess he had enough venom pumped into him to kill six men,' Malmuddy commented. 'He probably suffered a seizure anyway.'

Duncan said, 'All the gold in the world will do him no good now, and I don't reckon he'll be entering heaven through the golden gates.'

'Let's bury him,' the reverend said, 'so his soul can receive judgment.'

20

The first leg of their journey home was tiresome but unremarkable. Always Laughing guided Duncan, Cooper, Malmuddy, Catherine and Simpson to the main village of the Osages. Big Horse and his people welcomed them with splendid hospitality. They rested there for three days, the doctor treated Duncan's swollen hand, and then they set out once more. They had been provided with fresh horses and again Always Laughing showed the way, this time to the outskirts of Pinto. Here she bade them farewell with heartfelt sadness.

The reverend embraced her, kissed her forehead and said he would forever remember her in his prayers. He had loved her as a father would love a daughter.

In Pinto they also said goodbye to

Doctor Malmuddy and Jake Simpson. The doctor had undergone experiences he would never forget or wish to repeat. His lust for gold had been completely cured. As for the diminutive Simpson, he was a strange man and he departed without expressing his intentions for the future.

Duncan sent a telegram, courtesy of Western Union, to the Texas Rangers' headquarters in Austin and had funds made available to pay for their travel home by sea. The following week, he, the reverend and a confused Catherine embarked on a steamer and enjoyed unbelievable comforts after the rigours of their experiences.

During the voyage, Duncan did his utmost to make Catherine believe that going home was the best thing for her. Reluctantly she came to agree.

* * *

Ten days later Emily Hennessey welcomed her daughter home with unrestrained joy. Duncan stood back while tears flowed and words of love were exchanged. Explanations and excuses might follow later, if they were needed. Presently, Emily drew back.

'You must come upstairs, my love,' she said to Catherine, then she turned to Duncan. 'Please . . . you as well.'

He started to decline, believing this to be a private matter, but Emily's insistent look had him changing his mind. He followed the couple up the grand staircase to the big bedroom in the front of the house.

Edward Hennessey was lying back in bed, a pale figure compared to his previous self, but his eyes brightened as they entered.

'Thank God,' he murmured, 'thank God you're home, Catherine. And welcome to you, Duncan.'

Catherine held back, hesitating. 'Father . . . you're not angry?'

He shook his head. He made an effort to sit up and Emily adjusted his pillows for greater comfort. 'I've been mighty close to death,' he said. 'Doc Carter had given me up for a goner. I proved him wrong — just. But it was a wake-up call and it made me see things clearer. I've got to face facts. I'll never be fit enough to run for Governor, nor anything else. But more important, I've realized how badly I treated you, Catherine. I was a bully. I made your life a misery. All that will change, I promise. I love you and I'm just so glad you've come home.'

Catherine burst into tears. She stepped forward and embraced her father. 'And I'll be a better daughter,' she sobbed.

Duncan stood with Emily Hennessey, slightly embarrassed but suddenly happy at this sign of affection.

When Edward at last drew back from his daughter's arms, he looked at Duncan and smiled. 'Of course, there'll be the matter of the reward,' he said. 'Never will money be better spent.' He extended his hand: Duncan walked over and shook it, feeling its frailty.

'The reward?' Duncan said. 'That must be spent on repairing the church in town. I guess the Reverend Cooper earned the reward more than anybody else.'

Edward nodded. He was too tired to ask for further explanation, but his elation at Catherine's return had been like a tonic for him. He leaned back, a contented smile on his face.

Duncan exchanged a glance with Emily Hennessey's tearful eyes, then he turned and went down the stairs. The mission had been achieved, but at terrible cost. Now he promised himself he would retire from the Rangers, turn to farming and concentrate on loving Mandy and little Lilly — a pleasure he hankered for more than anything else in the world.

THE END